DINNER AT GORHAM'S

DAVID J. KENNEY

David J. Kenney

ISBN-13:978-0-9981605-0-4

CONTENTS

Author's Introduction

This book is. It offers no judgements or lessons on anything. It is a simple narrative based on imaginings. The author wrote it in winter for himself during a time of dreary weather and boredom. The book is not aimed at any delineated audience. Almost certainly none such exists.

This story narrates the young womanhood of a bright and handsome woman from St. Petersburg. She decides in a trice to leave the world of her childhood and university for the world "out there". She is not coddled. The book's early settings are St. Petersburg, Moscow, Yasenevo, Denmark and Northern Germany.

After immigrating to the United States she works at Harvard and on Nantucket and lives in Boston and on the Island. The story concludes as she settles into a life that rewards her and nearly exhausts her talents.

The author's labor created a disorderly draft and the readability of the final text depends greatly on the editing of Amy Elizabeth Davis. Amy masquerades as a historian, but for one of her guild knows more about the English language than almost all others.

Brittany Hooper, of Pam Owens Design and Gerry Quinn gilded the covers with their high competences. The author swam and sailed in those waters with good results.

It goes without saying that any married author living en famille must credit his or her spouse. So it is here. Justine has acceded to long silences and sudden walks and on occasion to the author's substantial consumption of liquids from Bordeaux and the Languedoc. Her wit and humor constituted a unique prod throughout.

David J. Kenney
Upperville, Virginia

CHAPTER 1

Preemption

"YOU DON'T fool me, Jilly."

"How's that Harry?"

"You are a hell of a lot more skilled then you let on. It's a good act. You have a boyfriend in Boston who drums up profitable computer jobs. Nobody visits you from the mainland, and we don't really know where you came from. But you get along.

"You're the person that people make room for in a crowded elevator. I think you discover passwords and infiltration points very quickly. I figure you get small accounts with big firms, hospitals, and investment banks, steal their data, and sell it to the highest bidder.

"Who is he Jilly, some old guy around State Street? He drums up business for you, and you give him sex?" He swigged his beer and sat back satisfied, as if he had discovered wrongdoing he was determined to punish unless he could profit from it. Jilly pondered the accusation. In his perverted righteousness, Harry had discovered the method, but not the target. Maybe Cotton Mather's sensitive radar for mischief still lurked in the Nantucket subconscious.

Jilly knew danger from her training, but Harry's threat was different, a bit of social awkwardness spoken by a drunken boob with a smarmy smile. It could halt her mission. Harry was fundamentally a coward, his bluster meant to incite liquid conversations. He would scheme, but without the sense to keep his clever idiocies to himself. "Why can't I be your agent, Jilly? I can bring you hundreds of hours of complicated work that would pay far more than you get from lawyers and doctors?" He leaned forward as though they were allies in common cause. The boat's bow left the water at the wave's crest, hesitated, and slammed down into the trough before the next swell.

JILLY REACHED into her bag as if hunting for a second beer. She opened her pricker and thrust it through Harry's left nostril into his frontal lobe. Death was instantaneous. Harry had no time to change his expression. Jilly had no discussion with her conscience. This was her third, excluding the Dag who was destined to make a predictable and lethal error and who drowned of his own accord.

The eighteenth-century Russian Admiral Ushakov beat the Turks time after time in the Mediterranean. He had found his natural losers. Harry belonged to the same

1

melancholy guild. She tied a rope around his neck and moved him over the side into the water. Lars had given her the pricker with the assurance that it could divide any rope, wire, or synthetic line in order to splice two strands together. She closed the pricker, opened the knife blade, and slit Harry's trunk from neck to navel. Water rushed in, blood and intestines jumped out. Jilly adjusted sail and steered directly into the storm. She took the line around Harry's neck and secured the end around the rudder post so the boat towed him in open water without leaving blood on the gunnels. A light rain fell, and the wind came up. The harbor master was sure to check which small boats were not visible from his perch.

Jilly sailed directly into the storm as the rain grew thicker. When she was sure she was beyond eyesight, she hauled Harry's body under the stern and cut the line from his neck. He did not look as if he had recently been alive. Baby sharks would consume his flesh, and the bones would sink to the bottom. The gravediggers could stack their shovels. Although the jaw held identifiable fillings, they would separate after a few days and the metal would sink into a prison of sand. She threw the line into the water. The sea was cold, and so was the rain. She put on her life jacket and sent up a flare. She used the only remaining flare five minutes later. She waited. The bridge watch on a forty-five-foot yacht saw it. The skipper increased speed, then cut his engines and closed to her windward side to give her some protection from the storm's increasing rage.

The yacht's deck hands threw fenders down to protect their boat from the prow of the sail boat. A small messenger line hit Jilly on the shoulder. She barely moved. A very tall blond man heaved a ladder over the side, climbed down, and secured the sails. He reached forward and tied a heavy line to the bull nose so that they could tow Harry Black's boat. He pushed Jilly up the ladder. She fell into the arms of a soaking wet sailor and collapsed.

AFTER JILLY was returned to shore, she could not speak coherently to her rescuers. Most aboard the yacht believed Harry's incompetence had betrayed her. Her story to the state police and the harbor master about the sad events of that day recounted every detail exactly—except for her having killed Harry and disposed of the body overboard. Harry's hangover, alcohol on his boat, his lack of a response to storm warnings, and his having only a single inexperienced crew member were all deemed to have contributed to his losing control of the boat in a worsening sea. Daring misfortune, he had dispensed with a life jacket even as the wind rose. No one questioned the events that led to Harry's death.

AT THE NECESSARY coroner's inquest, Jilly wore dark glasses to cover her swollen face. Her gait was halting, her tan attenuated. A stern and disinterested judge presided. She searched vainly for misbehavior on Jilly's part, but found none. The judge had a public face five days a week, contemplative, firm and precise. Appeals of her judgments were rare. She lunched with her clerk, the assistant district attorney, and the sheriff. From Friday eve to Monday morning, she skulked alone in an alcoholic haze.

Jilly knew something of the woman's life, which was not a secret from the islanders. I work for a government too, but I live a clandestine existence and must be seen daily as bright, mildly eccentric, friendly, and open to sailing with barely competent crew. I am a Russian and must make friends with almost everybody I meet. The judge is an American, yet she remains distant from all but her subordinates.

Charlie Banks, the attorney who had presided over the purchase of Jilly's house sat to her left, standing sometimes with folded arms, ever watchful, and as attentive as a solicitous parent. Mindful that a death by sailing boat might prejudice the tourist trade, the magistrate kept the proceedings short and requested the newspapers on Cape Cod and in Boston not cover they story. They complied, printed nothing, and waited for bigger fish. No fault was found. The magistrate declared Harry's death accidental. She advised Jilly to sail with more competent companions. Only one scarcely rude comment was heard about Harry. An old fisherman stood on the church's steps after the memorial and stage whispered; "the fish are no safer today than before Harry's passing. He almost never caught one, couldn't get the hook out without stabbing himself and if he did he let the fish squirm away."

HARRY'S BODY was never found. For a time, the islanders missed the five minutes of mindless buffoonery he offered to anyone who would listen. As for Jilly, she admitted to herself that she had neither liked nor disliked Harry and that one's own survival is a valid reason for killing. She had gotten past her first brush with American jurisprudence, and no fingerprints or DNA sample taken. Krushkin, the man who had sent her to America, was correct. The unexpected in a foreign culture caused the heart to beat faster than normal. She had acted her part well. Much of it was not acting.

CHAPTER 2

Dinner at Gorham's

SEVERAL MONTHS EARLIER, Jedidiah Gorham had opened his red door as Jilly ducked under the thorns sprouting from an archway of roses. "Come in, my dear. It's cold out there." Ever the banker, he shook her hand with a firmness meant for large depositors. He closed the door against the rain and invited her into a chilly living room. The other guests were sitting on straight backed chairs. Charlie Banks, an affable if reserved lawyer, seemed stuck to the wall, leaning against cream wallpaper whose origins were unknown. It had skirted the living room for so many years that no one commented on its portrayal of ships under sail in a tumultuous storm.

Charlie smiled at everyone, spoke handsomely with all who approached, and looked over his friends as a bishop over his flock. He encouraged those he knew to be in distress, congratulated those who had minor triumphs, and intervened when he saw hostile parties about to engage in serious disagreement. He did not flirt with wives or girlfriends. He did not drink excessively except on New Year's Eve and always complimented the wine and the food. He was the perfect guest and friend. Charlie had been counsel for the Bank of Sconset and the Gorham family since his days as a clerk in Boston. How delightful, Jilly thought, to sit with decent if boring dinner partners. This was a step up from the Saturday night orgies in the Sluzhba gymnasium.

There, just after Saturday dinners, staff, students, and administration had assembled in small bands during the designated "Recreational Activities" in the posted weekly plan. They circled each other menacingly until women, beer, petty dislikes, gambling debts and the frictions of the week incited brawls. At Jilly's last Saturday night get-together, two female corporals cut each other over supposed differences in office behavior. There was probably more to it than that. A burly sergeant broke his opponent's arm as they wrestled under a table. Nobody had a clue why. No records were kept of injuries or unmilitary behavior on those evenings. A medic stood by like a ghost, his presence neither ordered nor recorded. He accepted payment in dollars and Euros.

IN EARLIER CENTURIES, the Gorhams' Great Room had served as a commodious place where the entire family could gather during winter storms. Two interlaced anchors hung over the fireplace. Ship models and yachting pictures, mostly of Gorham whalers

4

and packets, dotted the walls. The nineteenth-century books filling the shelves told of ancestors' whaling expeditions, which had set out from Nantucket to profit handsomely or lose everything.

"The last Gorham who made a life at sea sailed on the Thomas Lawson, the only seven-masted ship ever built. It was constructed in New Bedford in 1898, meant for the lumber trade, but it didn't capture enough cargo to fill its massive holds and failed commercially. It eventually crashed ashore in 1923 on the Scily Islands, and everyone aboard died. After her, we became lawyers and bankers. But we always came back to the island."

The unfeigned sincerity of Jed Gorham's recitation captured Jilly. He loved his family's myths and Nantucket itself as much as he did his bank's profits. He especially wanted to vaunt the island's history to his newest find, whom he did not know to have been born in Saint Petersburg. Her true name was Katerina Michailovna Obrazova.

"Too hot if we light a fire, too cold if we don't. What is a man to do? Drink, I guess." The banker laughed. His six-foot wife smiled respectfully. She and her family had known Jed's for generations, and nothing about her needed to change for her to take her place as the banker's junior partner. She had been born on the island, schooled in New Haven, and knew the tight smiles that passed for humor in both. In middle age, Jed had come to love his wife for more than her surfeit of voting stock in the bank. She had always admired him. Now, in middle age, life without him was unthinkable. Jillian sat back, sipped her drink, and tried to enjoy Jedidiah Gorham's feeble attempts at bonhomie. He was a decent man, in no way a dissembler, but he was most at ease in front of a computer screen that displayed his increasing wealth.

Jilly knew that she had been invited because of the two-hundred-thousand dollars she had placed in his bank for a down payment on her house. Few newly arrived single women could afford such an elegant, albeit small, cottage. Besides, she was a trim well-muscled young woman who dressed for acceptance rather than seduction. She walked strongly, swung her arms with purpose, and carried her groceries out of the Stop and Shop with ease. Like many other islanders, she took her own bags to her bicycle and hired a local to mow her lawn. She could not chance roiling that small and insidiously curious society.

When not pondering deposits and loans, Jed imagined Jilly's body straining at his boat's coffee grinder as she brought in sail at a storm's rising. A woman like that had to have a man in her life. Who was he? Where was he? Jed Gorham and the room wanted to know.

JILLY HAD BEGUN to receive invitations from the island's great and good soon after she arrived on Nantucket at Thanksgiving, and then came small but lucrative computing jobs for doctors, travel offices, and ferry boats struggling with paper accounts and record keeping. Some saw their businesses portrayed realistically for the first time. One captain had three years supply of fuel but only enough lube oil for a few cruises.

She rarely entertained, yet others wanted her easy company. She had come to know the island's permanent hierarchy by winter's end. One elderly man claimed Cotton Mather as his fellow alumnus, and another described his trip around Cape Horn by the mast. She recognized the name Mather, but she had not experienced the hazards of the Horn.

JILLY HAD EARNED her fifteen minutes of fame quickly. A yacht owner who leased his boat to hedge-fund operators and billionaires dressed up a dinner by inviting Jilly to the Yacht Club and seating her next to a wealthy Japanese executive who arrived in a blue suit, white shirt, dark tie, and a white yachting cap that he reluctantly removed before dinner. They exchanged meaningless pleasantries before Jilly realized that his awful breath prevented the propinquity that enjoyable conversations demand. He soon realized that she was wearing a skirt longer than he had anticipated. Undaunted, he tried to pull it up far enough to reach her thighs.

She returned his self-satisfying smile, rose, took his dish of strawberries and cream, and poured it over his head. Strawberry juice flowed down his white shirt and chilled his navel. He rose, bowed twice to his hosts, found his yachtsman's cap, and bolted. He was not seen ashore or on his rented yacht for the remainder of the port call, remaining confined until the boat lay beyond territorial waters. Jillian became the talk of Main Street and was thenceforth known as the enterprising woman who put that foreign weasel in his place. A gray-haired man, quite old, thin, and in good clothes stopped her one afternoon. "I understand that you had an awkward moment at dinner the other night."

Jilly put on a serious face. "Well, I suppose you might say that. And you are?"

"Doesn't matter. I wish only to congratulate you. You did splendidly. You give me hope for the younger generation." He tipped his hat and moved away. Jilly walked to her bicycle and pondered the small size of the island.

HER BUSINESS DOUBLED, and suspicion about her character and purpose lifted. She had crossed the border from new and respectable to virtuous eccentricity, joining a diaphanous world that was difficult to enter, easy to leave, and much admired by the islanders, rich and poor. The inquest confirmed Jilly as Charlie's friend, a relationship that many coveted and some earned.

CHAPTER 3

Katerina Michailovna Obrazova

KATERINA MICHAILOVNA had always stood apart and, mostly, above. After shining at St. Petersburg University, she jumped a few rungs on the ladder to head a group of trade analysts. The others were easy to ignore but companionable enough to share two long desks in their windowless room. One rarely changed her dress, with predictable results. "Good morning, Katerina Michailovna" and "Good night, Katerina Michailovna" was all she ever heard from her dour trio of assistants.

She wrote algorithms that predicted commodity prices sooner and faster than the companies' managers. Her boss could barely understand her work. He whined constantly that he didn't know how to answer questions about Katerina's data, which he sent on to oil and shipping corporations.

The runner who brought her work orders walked like the stooped and withered peasant he was. Even before Afghanistan, he could neither hear nor speak easily. Then a large piece of shrapnel had sliced off an eye and an ear. Nobody looked at him.

One cold Wednesday afternoon, he brought Katya two brown envelopes. The first contained her next assignment. The second contained a one-way ticket to Moscow and instructions to pack enough for several days. It included an address, but no information about where she was going or where she would stay for the several days. That and the one-way ticket seemed ominous. All the envelope was missing was a note on which someone had scrawled the old Sluzhba expression Vsew budet yasno (All will be clear). She wasn't so sure.

KATRINA KNEW LITTLE of her family and had little family to leave behind. She had been two when her mother died in the waiting room of a St. Petersburg hospital after a car accident, and her father had done the best he could to raise her. One grandmother had survived combat, been decorated for her service as an Ohotnika, sniper during the Battle of Leningrad, and died of typhus soon after the war. She knew less of her other grandparents. They were probably buried in the collective grave of some distant village. 'Yes," her father said whenever she asked, "they died." Nothing else.

Her father worked in Vasilevski Island on ballistic missilery. His mathematical skills were legend and had earned him a large apartment where he practiced the eccentricities prohibited him during the day, shuffling around the two bedrooms, kitchen, and large living room of the flat his position had earned him. At home, he lived in a droopy sweater tattered by a thousand attacks from Isaac, the cat. Katya, who had become his best friend after she learned to read, lived two floors below in a smaller and less elegant flat.

Often asked to lecture in the West, he refused unless ordered by the Kremlin in one of its attempts to dazzle the its adversaries. "Let them paint their own walls," he would say. His collection of modern art was so awful that Katya had accused him of buying for the Technical Institute in Omsk.

HIS REAL TRIUMPHS came on Sundays, when he prepared lavish meals for ten or twelve of the physicists and mathematicians he worked with. Katya wore her best dress, curtsied when they entered, hovered over them, and served them food they could never purchase on their own. Her father had access to the special stores for the nomenclatura in Moscow and Saint Petersburg—shops where luxury was available at modest prices. Fyodor and Gennady, the only remaining Marxists in the group, always bowed to Katya when they arrived. They hurried to the great table, heaped their plates with zakuski (hors d'oeuvres), and grunted satisfaction to each other. They both ate like hungry Romanovs, and left nothing on their plates.

"Better than before? Gennadi?"

"Oh yes, Arkady much better."

None of these men had been left unscarred by the Great Patriotic War. A collapsing building had crushed the right leg of the shorter Marxist, who refused a cane and dragged the leg as if it were a decoration. All had lost many relatives in their parents' generation. A few had lost their entire families. Sitting with others of the same fate connected them to an unmourned age. They were content. Those old men and Katya's friend Olga Filipova had been there for her as she grew from the miseries of a motherless adolescence to the joys of a beautiful body ordered by a disciplined and searching mind.

OLGA FILIPOVA had been born in Ryazan, a bit southwest of Moscow, just as the German retreat began. After her family was killed, she survived alone in what barns and hovels remained after the to and fro of the Russian and German armies. Her village ceased to exist. It was indistinguishable from the burned fields that surrounded it.

When Olga was five-years-old, she walked the fields barefoot, searching for potatoes or corn to feed herself and her cousins. She grew up weak, but pretty and affable. An army officer in the chemical corps stationed in the city found her, danced with her, and married her. He left the army for graduate studies and became a wonder of sorts in the scientific community on Vasilevski Island. Katya's father knew him and invited him to his Sunday lunches.

Olga Filipova, who was childless, took a motherly took an interest in Katya. She taught her how to dress and how to tie the cascading ribbon in her hair that well-brought up girls wore. She wept with Katya at the girl's first broken love. They established a friendship that among Russians lasts a lifetime. Katya drove her father's car when they shopped, as much to help the arthritic old lady as to show off her driving skills.

Once, well into autumn, they passed a line of pedestrians in front of a store. "Ostan seichas! Stop Katya. Valenki! Boots!" Olga erupted from the car, crossed the avenue through traffic, and made for the line. A scuffle broke out. Men and women lost their hats and bags. It took police to put the line back in order. Twenty minutes later a triumphant Olga returned to the car holding a pair of high fur-topped boots. "Now the snow can come." During her university years and afterwards, Katya bought Olga winter boots at the Special Store. She used her father's ID card. The guard winked. At each winter's end, she took the boots back from her friend and, used though they were, gave them to one of her nearly indigent classmates from the ethnic republics.

NOW, KATYA would be forbidden to write to her old friend and guardian. That winter's day, she packed a small bag and took the Metro to Moscow Station. An incomprehensible force pricked her legs to climb the greasy black steps onto the train. She met the fug of smoke, unbathed bodies, and sweaty tea woman with a mustache with irritation.

The dreary tracks and the anonymously sent ticket frightened her. The mixture of rain and soot from passing locomotives gave the car's windows ugly streaks. There was little comfort in watching wet snow turn the ice to mud and then back again as the night destroyed what was left of the daylight's warmth. The people outside were barely moving black dots. Did everybody in Northern Russia walk hunched over from an invisible cross? The tea lady lurched down the aisle, and Katya bought a mug of tea, mostly to distract herself from the troubling brown envelope with its one-way ticket. Her life had been a chain of certainties; a good apartment, a doting father, successful student life and a job well above the positions her friends had gotten. On the train, she realized that for the first time she did not know what she did not know.

CHAPTER 4

Sluzbha

THE TICKET'S ARRIVAL screamed Sluzhba, the secret organization that became heir to the Cheka after the demise of the Soviet Union. The Cheka had been born when Lenin issued a simple decree to expand his police force from the confines of St. Petersburg to the entire Soviet Union. The Cheka, her father explained, was not a commisia that talked about things but a commissariat that accomplished concrete and specific goals upon orders from one or two of the Vashni, the important ones within the Kremlin.

The Sluzhba had inherited its two critical missions, both aimed at "All Union." The first covered everyone within the country's boundaries, which incorporate the ethnic republics—anyone could be confined indefinitely, and all were subject to intrusive interrogation and surveillance. Any Russian traveling alone in foreign countries was a potential defector. The second was defense of the border. The Sluzhba had its own small navy, air force, and army. Duty there was considered a sign of low intelligence, a sin against an instructor, or a desire to remain in Russia. But it was often exciting, and a few were killed every year.

Katya's father offered cautionary tales and enough folk wisdom that she knew how to stay out of the Sluzhba's glare. He had greater freedom. His contributions to the missile program had always given him some immunity from the snoopers as he climbed the ladder of success on Vasilevski Island. Still, the close surveillance by the Sluzhba outside the USSR inhibited him from attending prestigious international conferences—he did not like being shepherded around in a security envelope. Even at a matey post-Gorbachev conference, a mousy security man inspected every room as they checked in and made sure that even prominent scientists were in their rooms by midnight. Her father found a shabby little man in his bedroom, patches of sweat still drying on his gray suit, and said softly, Dostatochno (enough). The man scuttled out, closing the door softly.

"YOUR GRANDMOTHER operated alone at night in the ruins of Leningrad and killed quite a few Germans. She was made Hero of the Soviet Union. Hers is the way I prefer. Operate alone and well concealed." He emphasized that the service's powers trumped the local police or militia and that it could watch anybody or anything in the country or beyond it. A farmer shorting bales of cotton in Kazakhstan could be arrested as easily as an American spy about to steal the Kremlin's code books. "Do not sell any of your precious algorithms to outsiders," he warned. "Your fingerprints are all over them. Every coder has an identifying style. Just like bomb makers."

Her father did not scald the regimes that had brought Russia near to extinction, near-abject poverty, and a sense of national despair. He was sad that it had happened and content that the days of monstrous evil were over. He and his students quietly produced great and meaningful work for their country. Their very obscurity brought them celebrity among those who mattered. He had made his way in a corrupt world with no reluctance, and if it owed him, he owed it. He had smiled and conquered the repressive habits of all the governments since the Second World War. He believed in his work, as he did in his daughter. Katya understood this. Leaving her father would bring her an unusual sadness, knives in both their hearts. They had never been apart.

STEPPING UP the greasy black steps into the hard car, she understood she was volunteering for risk of a kind she could not predict. A fear that differed from her pre- examinations jitters and a profound loneliness that came from already missing her father took over her consciousness. No calming algorithm suggested itself.

CHAPTER 5

In Training

THE INSTRUCTIONS in the brown envelop were precise. Early train to Moscow, Metro to . . . Walk two blocks west on. . . to the eight-story building on the right and present yourself no later than 1 p.m. on Monday, 13 April. Katya opened the wooden door. Inside, a middle-aged woman with wattles reaching almost to her chest sat behind a desk. An armed guard stood by the side of a narrow door of painted steel. There were no identifying marks anywhere. The walls were bare. The bleakness almost overcame Katya's trepidation. The woman glowered and demanded her name. Soon the guard beckoned, opened the steel door, and led her down a passage wide enough for three people abreast. He knocked on a green door and entered. Katya followed.

A handsome older woman dressed from the shops on Nevski Prospect smiled and told her to sit. The guard left. The woman spoke into the telephone, Ona prishla (She's here). She rose and opened a blue door. "Please" she gestured. Katya entered. A fortyish man with good bones, a Saville Row suit, and a modish hair cut rose and shook her hand.

"WELCOME, KATERINA Michailovna. Please sit down. We have heard such wonderful things about you that we thought you might consider being of higher service to the state than your present job allows. You come from a line of patriots."

Katya wondered if her father were ordering her through a surrogate. "My name is Vadim, not that it will be of any consequence to you. Most people call me Comrade V behind my back. But we are all friends here, so it really doesn't matter. By the way, don't worry about your boss. He believes the computer people here want you for a few days of classified work."

He settled back behind the finest Moldavian oak desk she had ever seen and smiled through his horn-rimmed glasses. She would never like him. He would never be a confidant. "The first stage is nothing that should bother you. You will remain inside the building for the moment, and you may not communicate with anyone, not even with your dear father, who is very busy anyway. He is working on something to do with our business. A real patriot from the old Russia is rare in these troubled times of change at the top, a new class of billionaires, and unrest—to put it politely—in the Ukraine. The nomenclatura is not what it used to be."

Shiny oak desks and London suits are rare, as they were in the old days, Katya thought. The man sounded like a tour guide. Yet his few words held a warning. Any misstep by Katya would redound to her father, no matter how respected he was. "You will have a busy week here. I won't keep you any longer." He pushed a button under his desk.

The door opened, and a tattooed giant entered. "This is Oleg. He was in the *Vory* (mob) at Norilsk and ratted on his mate. The head of his particular union tried to execute him. Oleg strangled the two who were sent to cut his throat. Because of certain physical skills, he was assigned to the psychiatric ward as an orderly. He makes no noise when he walks because he continues the practice of wearing the felt slippers required in the asylum. The regular city police want to execute him for anti-state activities, which means that he killed some cops. So we took him in. It's the only safe place for him. He is very gentle, very intelligent. He will explain our routine, answer questions, and take you to your room."

She took a pen from his desk and signed a document not meant to be read. Vadim looked up, conveying menace rather than the end of a job interview, and offered his hand. "One more thing. No names are ever used in this building except for a few like my own. Your new identification is #75." He smiled and waved her out with contemptuous languor.

OLEG ESCORTED her from the room. He turned left down a hallway with no apparent end and spoke in a soft voice. *Somewhere from Northern Siberia, she thought, from the tribal areas, no education, but he's picked up a vocabulary.* The small waves of fat above his collar disguised his tattoos. "75, there are a few directions for your stay here. When we arrive at your room, put all your clothes and personal things in the bag provided. Put on the trainers, underwear, and gym clothes that hang on the wall. These will be replaced every two days. There is no key to your room. It locks automatically in the evening at ten and opens every morning at six. Your day begins at 6:10 in the gym. Directions are painted on the floor. There are no phones or intercoms.

"Arrows on the floor lead to the cafeteria. Avoid conversation. You can ask for the salt and pepper. I will wait outside while you change into your new clothes." He began to close, then reopened the door halfway. "One more thing, 75. There is a GPS in one of your shoes. Should you get lost, we can find you and bring you back."

A bed, small wooden desk, and chair filled her entire room. An iron toilet was welded into the corner. The room's occupant could hang no pictures, choose no furniture, or arrange none of the oddments that accumulate through life. In its way, it was mathematically perfect, designed to set the limits of a certain existence without pain—unless its occupant were claustrophobic. *My God,* she thought. *A father's good reputation and university success shouldn't lead to this.* The one-way ticket lingered in a little nest of anxiety all its own. She fell asleep before the lights went out.

THE STERILITY of the first week fascinated her. "No mix of colors or architectural styles" she mumbled to herself on the way to breakfast. No great buildings loomed out of the dissipating fog on the riverbank. The air carried no scent, neither exhaust fumes nor salt from the Baltic. She looked for, but never found, 74 or 76. Determining the size of the group was impossible. The substantial number of women surprised Katya. "They'll soon be busy," she whispered to 89.

Her tablemates had not lived near the seats of scientific power, and one of them trembled when asking for the salt. Some were pure Russians. A few came from Kazakhstan, Siberia, from near the Chinese border, and even Dagestan. The food came in large quantities to compensate for its dullness. Her father would call it stodge, an all-encompassing phrase he'd picked up while lecturing against his will at Oxford, where his closet door opened onto a brick wall. An MI-6 joke, he thought. Later he concluded that some people lived that way.

75'S WEEK EXHAUSTED her as much because of its difference from her usual routine as from its sixteen-hour days. There were no breaks. No morning coffee or gossip in the cafeteria at lunch. For a desk worker, morning calisthenics brought pain to unused muscles. Every night, she wrote answers to the questionnaires left in her room by an unseen hand. Could she live alone without family for long periods? Was she comfortable meeting new people, confronting different languages and dialects, what surprised or disturbed her, did she want children? Some of the questions had a military taint. Did she like guns or other kinetic weapons? Had she ever hunted? Would she kill if she were in peril? She decided that she would. None of this was linked to her academic skills, her three coworkers, or the disfigured man who delivered her orders. By the end of the third day, she missed them all. She missed her father most, and she missed the smells and the warmth of those Sunday lunches.

CHAPTER 6

Yasenevo

AFTER A WEEK of tests, she received a note advising her that she had been selected for training in the Sluzhba. She was admonished that her commissioning as an officer and a choice first assignment depended on her successful completion of the academic and practical work that lay ahead. Failure would remand her for two years in the army. 75 boarded a bus with worthless springs to head east of Moscow to Yasenevo and a cluster of low concrete buildings, windowless on the first floor, tiny but with tiny slitted openings on the second. No trees or flower beds greeted them. The buildings clawed at the land. Only barbed wire on a high wall and a machine-gun post at a heavy metal gate told the observer that the compound sheltered military activities. Plowed strips two-hundred meters wide surrounded the walls. *The buildings probably shift in the winter and spring. They couldn't build higher than two stories,* she thought. The treeless land was open to grant its occupants a clear field of fire, her tactics instructor later told her. She never learned who the attackers might be.

Her room at Yasenevo raised the comfort bar. She had a closet and a normal, if spare, bathroom. She could open her door. Two sets of soldiers' fatigues, boots, gym shoes, and underwear sat on the bed. There were also heavy clothes, two sets of Arctic underwear, and woolen socks. She learned later that she was expected to steal or otherwise acquire other clothes and accessories that she might need or want.

IN THE BEGINNING, military training took precedence over classroom instruction. 75 endured firing pistol, rifle, and machine gun with patience. The weapons were greasy and smelled it. Physical training was hard. Jumping over obstacles threatened shorter students, which included most of the women, with being impaled on barriers' pointed sticks. She hated the chug-chug noise of mortars. After several too many grimaces, a scarred old sergeant took her aside. He warned her that "such displays would prejudice her final grade in small-unit tactics."

Military exercises were conducted in the mud, irrespective of the season, except when they led into dense forests where birds and bugs flew into exposed tissue at the slightest provocation. History lessons on the greatness of the Sluzhba, its successes, and the mortal vengeance it pressed upon its enemies took up more time than any student found entertaining. 39 dared one day to ask if the lectures were history or propaganda, but no one answered. Still, listening allowed them to sit and doze off. If the students left mud on the lecture hall's floor when they should have removed their dirty boots, a student was chosen by lot to clean up after supper. It took three hours.

A notebook stamped 75 on the cover lay on her desk in the bare classroom where introductory lectures on the glories of old Russia were peppered with tales of the Decembrists, Herzen's intellectual bravery, the turmoil of 1905, and minor acts of the masses on their march to socialism. The siege of Leningrad, the battles of Stalingrad and Kursk, and the fortitude of the Russian people hovered between the lines of most of the lectures. Sweating in his wool uniform, a slight figure rose: "Comrade Instructor. How did we win the siege of Leningrad?" Katya stage whispered: "Because of people like Grandma Sniper, you fool." Many heard, but did not turn. Students were ordered to become protectors of the revolution and of the people. The old Marxist cant insinuated itself into most of the lessons.

Midway on the third day, a big-bellied general came into the room without an introduction, although the medals on his lapels announced he had accomplished much. His huge body diminished the lectern. The instructors stood in silence along the walls. His burnished sentences rumbled up from deep within his chest to reinforce the menace of his words: "In the face of disaster, and it is inevitable, do not fail Russia, yourself, or your colleagues in the Sluzhba. If you or your mission face a lethal quandary, either you or your seniors have erred. In ninety percent of such situations, your training will tell you what to do and what not to do. The rest of the time, your instincts must guide you. In the field your colleagues you and you colleagues must trust one another. Duplicity is for the enemyYou must dig yourself out of whatever hole you have fallen into. Resolution will depend on you alone. After all this expensive training we do not want you to die in the Burmese jungle or rot away in a Kenyan prison."

HER FELLOW STUDENTS at Yasenevo envied 75'scomputer training. She had singular skills. "How do you know all these things 75?" asked 48, who served as the information Center of the class. If 48 didn't know of it, a strain of gossip did not exist. "I picked them up from my uncle," 75 replied. "He had a job repairing the boxes. He steered me toward a tech school where I learned how to fix the boxes and comprehend the software." Absent code clerks, computer operators in embassies and consulates often sent classified messages to the Center and deciphered those from Moscow. There was little they and the code clerks did not know about successes and failures in their parishes and who was sleeping with whom. 75 took a malicious delight in joining an elite inside the elite. That trumped the loyalty nonsense.

The students gossiped not only about themselves but about those out in the world. Most knew that many senior officers of the old Sluzhba were now rapacious entrepreneurs, more than a few had become billionaires. Those still in training got hints of their wheelings and dealings because former students sometimes used the school for conferences and confidential negotiations. They were isolated from Moscow's delights and intrusions. They knew which few rooms did not have listening devices. They knew how many dollars or Swiss francs were needed to secure the cooperation of the right person at the right time in the right place. One result of the success that these alumni demonstrated was that many of 75's classmates believed their training at Yasenevo would lead them to wealth and trips to the Cayman Islands. "How can those billionaires buy half of London and remain untouched while we get miserable salaries and lousy beds?" 9 bleated. 75 knew that the school's administration wanted the students to learn about the pseudo-defectors so that they could work among them and if necessary, harass them out of business. Or kill them.

On the other hand, the malodorous taint of the Cheka still hovered. The incumbents were equally as cruel and corrupt, in their way, as the prewar minions of Yezhov. The notion that any Russian living abroad was a potential defector or traitor still pervaded the thoughts and practices of the service's old-time officers. The rare denunciation still occurred, although exceptions were made in the treatment of rich exporters and their sons who bought stocks on the London and New York markets. A security team of one or more ill-dressed and diffident autocrats prowled around every embassy and consulate. Sometimes a sleeper emerged to denounce an embassy staffer who would be isolated and flown back to Moscow the next day, where his or her family would also be interrogated and kept in their flat until the matter was settled. Sometimes, the accused was exonerated to prove that justice existed. 75 was sure that a sleeper lived among her classmates. She thought after a few weeks that she had discovered him.

THE WEEKS ROLLED ON, punctuated by a few brawls fought out of boredom and a few unusually brilliant lectures. There were more of the former. 75 sidled up to 44 after a German movie to ask "44, why did you punch 11? You hurt him and broke his glasses."

"75! Intellectuals have no place here. What if he broke or dropped his glasses climbing into a second-story office? Would he fumble with the latch or take the time to recover his glasses? He has no future with us."

Several of the women, competent seamstresses, mended clothes and collars and heavy underwear in exchange for cigarettes or beer that had been liberated during the weekend parties. These were exchanged for chocolate, sex, and the little obligations that make organizations function smoothly. It worked on the outside, they thought, why not on the inside.

75 could no longer find a nook in the Hermitage or ditch in a hayfield in which to secure temporary refuge. Work, exhaustion, and occasional brutality replaced the chaste monotony of calculating foreign trade. Within months, all the trainees had entered that impalpable state of the Russian mind, acceptance. Those who had entered thinking they were participating in a charade were brought down, their bubbles of frivolity pierced. Those who had lived in a shell were opened up by the strenuous

exercises and the need to depend on others. Almost all realized that they lived beyond their own kind.

The close combat instructor threw 75 onto the mat harder than she thought necessary and hurt her back. He grinned after each fall. She took a deep breath and smiled back. Students settled their squabbles in peace, whether sooner or later. Most were too tired to argue. When their disagreements escalated to open flesh, instructors and guards stepped in with little mercy for either party. When two male students were found entwined, the interrogation focused in part on the possibility of others. Because the student body ate, walked, marched, and studied in groups, the staff was anxious to know when and how they had formed their relationship.

The commandant got no answers, but in the meantime, someone had squealed about the problem to Moscow. The commandant did his best to leave as small a paper trail as possible. He blamed the chief of security for inadequate supervision of the students and certified that no breach of security had occurred. A guard was found guilty of culpable negligence, removed from his easy routine of counting people in and out, and assigned to burn the garbage and refuse from the entire compound. One evening after dark, guards escorted the unfortunates, who were barely able to walk, to small buses. They would be cast out onto the big cities' streets with no future except as rent boys.

75 STUDIED GERMAN in the language lab; hours of repetition gave her a north German accent. She guessed she might get an operational assignment in German or Austria. *Not what I want, but nearer than Djakata to father and the dacha.* In the classes on photography and listening devices, she ended up teaching her chums more than the instructors ever could.

That she came to like the outdoors and the increasingly rigorous physical requirements surprised her. She learned to swim. She was invited to join weekend orgies inside the compound's gymnasium, but declined. "Thank you, 22. I am satisfied where I am." She took a lover, a captain in the training department who was sufficiently senior to ward off others' aggressive demands for her favors. She was beautiful, he thought, and a shade taller than most Russian women and all the ethnics. Both knew it was a matter of convenience. Neither found himself wanting conversion to the language of love.

She became almost bilingual in German and a competent critic of post-1917 Russian literature." You know, 69," she said to her best friend, "I am studying all the stuff they taught at Pete. But I never knew the Americans had a constitution written in the eighteenth century and have two parliaments." Although her studies satisfied her curiosity, she was unable to keep up with high-level developments in the computer world. No learned journals arrived, nor did she ever get to see exhibition catalogues from the museums. These losses annoyed her. "Well, I made a choice," she mumbled in the shower, soaping herself with what seemed like cleaning fluid. Her monthly letter to her father was cleared before she stamped it.

She was more irritated than intimidated by the so-called street work. The bumping and jostling of thousands of people in a crowded city irritated her. Once she was asked to trail a Chechen troublemaker in Kiev. He had a good sense of danger. He found it impertinent that a young girl in a good coat dogged him. She turned a corner and found him waiting with a tire iron. Those supervising the exercise intervened just in time. "You are not yet ready for East London, devushka (young lady)." After another venture, in Odessa, she was asked how many trailers she had spotted. She had missed four of the seven following her, including a woman with a baby in a basket and an old man selling Cold War medals.

She had no vacations until the first summer. Then, she was given two weeks leave and allowed to visit her father in Sochi. The greeted each other silently, as if all were known about the other. 75 noticed her father still smiled as he always had but walked with a slight stoop and worked with less agility as they weeded his beloved garden. They ate no meat, only soups and vegetables from his plot. He had extended its size by bribing an old railroad boss who had settled in Sochi while in good health and immediately suffered a stroke that kept him imprisoned in a wheel chair. 75 lived in a silent dream. She got a tan. They slept and awoke early. When it was time, they parted without words at the train station. Neither set a date for their next meeting. They knew they had lived two weeks, a sign of a unique bliss that few would have.

CHAPTER 7

Student

75 KNEW HER INTELLIGENCE and skills set her apart. The military assignees and tedious young scientists feared the instructors and worried about their chances for a plum assignment at the end. But whenever an especially stern instructor hit 75 with a complicated question, she answered logically, simply, and without anxiety.

The students formed alliances; intelligence and presumed political connections provided the most important currency. University graduates generally scorned those with no advanced training; those from the military kept to themselves and protected each other. Two had been in the Spetnaz and were feared by the staff. Most of the students sensed which of them would find posting as a Sluzhba guard on the Finnish border and who would get a headquarters job or an assignment abroad. The instructors asked students with party connections easy questions.

The room they called La Salle Chinoise held mysteries untold. It seemed that an instructor had been returned from Hanoi with an intense and constant need for opium. His assignment to Yasenevo, away from the Center and from his native city of Kiev, was intended as his punishment. He claimed expertise in the matter of the illicit substances he imported, consumed, and traded. He asserted the best product originated in a few spots in southwest China whose village heads he knew. It surprised no one that the Russian underground economy functioned over thousands of kilometers, across state borders, and through the gates of Yasenevo. Whatever trouble he had caused in Hanoi, this intrepid descendant of Silk Road traders maintained a string of knowing contacts to keep him supplied. Whenever he invited her, 75 demurred.

THREE NIGHTS A WEEK, the students watched movies in English, French, German, and Spanish. 75 became sufficiently interested in the United States that she lip-synced the actresses' lines in the often-repeated detective films. The movies taught 75 about the pop culture of America and Europe, and at the end of a year, she preened that she could take the London underground and the New York subway without causing undue notice. The nerds at the language lab were not so sure.

British life intrigued her. She saw films of Shakespeare plays and tales of espionage. She read assigned pieces about the prodigious success of Kim Philby and Guy Burgess, Stalin's Englishmen. An old man approached her as she left a lecture on their cases.

"This is your inheritance, 75; we expect the same from you." He was pompous, but she assumed from his crutches that he had earned the right to be eccentric by serving in Afghanistan. Actually, he had been beaten up in Washington.

She found it incredible that no one had discovered and prosecuted Philby and his coconspirators for their treachery against Queen and Country. Spies were trained to discover hostile compatriots, no matter how charming or well educated. She concluded that unmasking Philby and his colleagues would have destroyed the social class into which he had been born and in which he had gained such favor.

The students' own self-possessed if easy baptism into the world of deceit got chilling validation from the school's CO, who ordered groups of them to name two trainees: the least competent and the most likely to defect. 75 and her crew had little difficulty in naming the least competent. 32 was a gangly fellow with hair as long as regulations permitted and a scar over his irregular nose. The prospective defector was harder to pick, but in the end they concluded unanimously that 6, glib, affable, always willing to buy beer for his mates, and skillful in Asian languages, was their candidate. He wore a Roman nose with Romanov pride and kept his blond hair meticulously combed. He would get along too well in the West. They sighed as though they were sewing a D on the back of his uniform.

Missing the colors of the great structures in Petersburg, the yellows and greens that were doubled by their reflections in the river Neva, she thought about the isolation of her new surroundings with disdain. How, she wondered one afternoon, could they train the young to defend Russia when they were isolated from the Russia of the soil and the snows. Where were its glorious past, nuclear missiles, and stinking factories? Looking around, 75 decided she would have ordered a great country house and farm built on one of the higher knolls. She dreamed that she would invite some of the Mariinsky ballet to dance for her on weekends. There was not a tree in sight and no falling leaves. Only the history-soaked damp earth of Russia gave off its singular smell. A bird lay dead in the plowed field beyond the gate.

AT LUNCH ONE DAY, 69 came rushing up to her table. "75 did you hear what happened to 55? Seems Comrade V's tests were not so accurate at picking out possible psychotics."

"No!"

"55 refused to leave the shower this morning. He screamed that he saw cockroaches on the wall and tried to kill them with his head. The guards came and ordered him to leave. He refused, and they sprayed him with riot gas. 22 saw him carried into the bus."

75 looked up from her fish. "It is sad, but I never liked him."

"Neither did I."

CHAPTER 8

Soldier

AWAY FROM YASANEVO, for a spell, students did their military and water training on Berezan Island, an experience even more arduous than they had become used to. Upon their arrival, the chief instructor reminded them that the traitor Lieutenant Schmidt of the Tsarist Navy had been caught and hung there in 1915. 75 had to prove every day that she could match or exceed the feats ex-footballers, gymnasts, and the few street thugs who had weaseled their way into the program on the basis of their fathers' positions or because a relative had a Sluzhba background. And that she did not intend to be hung here.

She became an expert swimmer in dry or wet suits and was once chosen to navigate for a platoon with two *Spetsnaz* instructors assigned to grade her. Her dry suit was too small and chafed her chest. She powdered her breasts, wrapped a discarded stocking around her chest, and moved with comfort. She ran up and down the sharp-edged cliffs with a twenty-kilo pack. A lean hardness replaced her soft figure. When the blister on her right heel broke during a downhill march, she did not stop. Bearing the pain was easier than absorbing the instructor's scorn.

One day, 2 tripped on a sharp rock, fell, and opened a large gash on his left thigh. The outflow of blood threatened to render him unconscious, and the instructor stopped the march to inspect the exsanguination. "Not bad, 2. You will survive. 75, you're a girl, you can sew. Can you do a cross stitch? I thought so. Wrap the cut now and sew him up tonight when we get back. You should learn how to deal with the unforeseen." No one on the march complained. If pain on these arduous hikes was certain, so was acceptance necessary.

Many of the swimming exercises were two-person trials designed to teach trainees to plant limpets, reconnoiter a beach, and crawl ashore to destroy a mock bridge. Pushing trainees beyond their capacity during the endurance swims was a favorite of a small, hard-faced Muscovite. "You will now," began the terrifying preamble to his instructions. The last place swimmer had to do twenty-five pushups before he or she was allowed supper. 12, an Uzbek, broke an ear drum after being held underwater for two minutes without oxygen.

One stormy afternoon, a hard-faced and competent marine emerged from the water, took off his gear, and rushed to the CO's office. He had navigated for 6, who swam the regulation three meters behind him. He looked back at the start of the swim and saw 6 swimming confidently. A few minutes later, after he made a 90-degree course change, the instructor realized 6 had missed the turn. A swift current created by a troubling storm, the worst in many years, had undoubtedly swept 6 away. Despite the gale, all the instructors took to the water but found nothing. No body or swimmer's gear ever turned up. Other than a change in protocol to require a third swimmer behind the navigator and student, no one commented on the misfortune.

In each class, a student selected by lot had to swim to the mainland and back with several large bottles of beer. In her group, it fell to 75. After her first two swims, she knew her navigation points, the lights, and the currents. She arrived at the far shore with her self-confidence immeasurably increased. She spent the night in a hut on the beach, her dry suit keeping her warm. After a stop the next morning at a near-deserted café where the night's survivors were still drunk, she returned to her mentors with two bottles of Baltika.

JUST BEFORE THE END of the military training, an especially nasty Dagastani instructor watched her from across the room. "Not bad" he grumbled through the bar's smoky haze. He was just sober enough to use his considerable strength. Rape was in the air, and she knew it. Her captain friend, visiting his wife and child in Moscow, could not protect her. As the thug whooped to his companions and turned to the bartender for another glass of lamentable vodka, she ran to her locker, put on her dry suit, and headed toward the boat dock.

He stumbled after her. *Bastard.* She waded into the water and aimed at the mainland, four-kilometers distant. Dressed in heavy civilian clothes, he fell into the waves and either drowned or expired from hypothermia. 75 didn't care which. After thirty seconds of gurgling and two thrusts of vomit, he was admitted by the sea as its reluctant guest. She swam for an hour to ensure she had no pursuers. She had rescued herself. She did not think any of the other instructors had even noticed she was missing.

NOT LONG AFTER, she received an envelope with a single page. "Special order #75. Bus to Sheremetyevo 1200. Flight 363M." In an old, noisy, propeller-driven transport she flew to Moscow, thence to Sevastopol, and went aboard a Sluzhba patrol boat for what her marine tutor called: "a realistic exercise of great value to a student." The crew had been informed that a female would come aboard to observe the mission. Smugglers were crossing the Turkish border into Russia with impunity. The regular border guards couldn't or wouldn't stop them. The realistic briefing given by the area's intelligence officer on what 75 could expect in the way of live rounds being fired in her direction (and what she might be called upon to do in reply) brought questions. Would she act in a military manner, freeze, or skulk in the rear? She called upon the spirit of Grand Mother sniper.

The captain, a senior lieutenant, put off at midnight and languished at sea until he received the time and place to land his troops and 75. The platoon she had joined jumped from their own hundred-meter wooden craft into motorized rubber boats, put the engines on silent slow, navigated through fog, and pulled up to the beaches. The commandos dug a beach defense line just inside the line of scrub outgrowth and waited until they saw flares at the top of the hill silhouetting the smugglers. Regular troops in the hills had arrived the previous night, dug in, and posted sentries to warn of the approaching smugglers. The army soldiers were well positioned to drive the smugglers toward the commandos and on their arrival to set off their flares. They would remain in their holes while the Sluzba troops advanced and killed.

The smugglers panicked and fled toward the beach into the trench line dug by 75's comrades. 75 shot one with her rifle. Her team captured the rest and put them in trucks that would bring them to Great Sochi for trial. The dead were left as a warning. One wounded man broke through the lines and confronted her. Her magazine was empty. She stared at him and he at her. She drew her pistol and shot him as he clawed at her face. An old soldier pulled her away from the body and down toward the beach.

"How did I do?" she asked a sergeant crouching beside her whose principal task that night was to keep 75 out of trouble. *Harasho* (well) he answered slowly and with sadness in his voice. 75's platoon suffered no fatalities and one superficial wound. They climbed into the rubber boats and motored silently toward the patrol boat flying the star and the crossed hammer and sickle. 75 was depressed and exhilarated. It was her first operation to result in blood. The captain took her weapons. He gave her his room on the way back.

75 FLEW TO MOSCOW and bused to Yasenevo. She brought an outstanding report of her valiant and professional behavior in combat. Later she sat silently on the edge of her bed. A few tears rolled down her right cheek. "My God, 69, I killed a man. Now I am one of them and not the daughter of a man whom I loved and who loves me. I can't serve his friends lunch or go shopping with Olga Filipova anymore. I can't even write to my father. Would they still love me and want me if they knew what I had done?"

69 replied quietly. "I think so. You grew up with them. They will never forget you. Not if you grow leopard's spots. Grandma sniper killed too, and she is an honored part of your family's history. Their thoughts about you are unchangeable. Whatever happens, you can always return to your extended family with grace. We are Slavs. We have a history. We live in history. We wallow in it and never change to suit the moment."

CHAPTER 9

Training Wheels

BACK AT THE COMPOUND, 75 delivered her congratulatory report to the commandant's office. Life proceeded, and the days brought small dramas. One student committed suicide, a few left voluntarily. Many were summarily sent away for reasons not always clear to their classmates. A very quiet man from the civil service in Omsk removed his clothes and walked mutely through the halls. After the duty officer spent fifteen minutes pleading with him to return to his room, he was restrained by force. Upon bending over in the shower, a very fit student was seen to have a tattoo impaled on the inner side of his right buttock. It marked its bearer as a member of one of the most brutal *Vory*, the gangs that ran most of the northern gulags. The young man, who claimed to be the son of a camp commandant, was dismissed to a site where he could do no harm. There, he would find it is very hot in summer and very cold in winter. The commandant called the entire school into the dining hall and ranted that "The staff could not accept a spy inside a school for spies." The students sat in muted acceptance. Once, one of the doors on 75's floor stopped opening at the prescribed time. When the room was reopened, it was clean of everything—including its occupant. Nobody explained why.

75 knew she was doing well. Her guile and soft manners shielded her from the scorn and punishments heaped on most the others. Without trying, she had become the unofficial favorite and trouble shooter among the students in that bare but perversely fascinating school cocooned away from the pains and privileges of twenty-first century Russia. 2 approached 75 after the night's movie. "I have a problem 75, and I need help. The soap we are issued is so strong that it reddens my face and scalp. It gets raw, and it often hurts. The canteen manager won't give me the better soap he keeps for the staff unless I screw him."

"You mean that bald piece of goat shit with the mustache?"

"That's the one."

Next noontime, 75 stood at the canteen and asked the manager for the lighter soap. "My father can get a few bars at his Special Store, but it will save time if I get them from you." He returned 75's request with a look of fear and loathing. He went to his storage room and returned with two bars of body soap and two bottles of hair shampoo. A few in the administration tried to knock her off her pedestal but failed.

Most reacted like the canteen manager.

THE PERMANENT INSTRUCTORS were locked into a life at Yasenevo, far from the sea and the world's glamorous cities, even as they trained their students to go out into that world. If most of the students chose only the life of blind obedience the instructors offered, so be it. For her part, rote training, insensitive and sometimes brutal, did not make 75 a rebel. But it did lead her to long for a different life. An especially loathsome instructor sneered: "How will you do in Lagos at night when you are cornered by a drug gang?" Her time at the Sluzhba school did not make her loyal to the new Russia.

Still, the mud-caked marches, small-arms practice, and surveillance had taught her skills that were universally useful. Her father and his contented friends would not live forever. All told, her feelings and intellect both told her it was time to leave the Russian bureaucratic umbrella. She loved Pushkin, the Mariinski Ballet, and the Hermitage. But the glories that had informed her early life were fading. The Americans had an apt expression: Take off the training wheels.

CHAPTER 10

Moscow and Exurbs

TOWARD THE END of the second year, the students were split up for further training. The more doltish would become Sluzhba border guards. Others were sent to learn domestic police work, anti-terrorism tactics, or to join other special units. A few would spy on the large organs of government or the defense establishment in order to keep the central bureaucracy abreast of potentially dangerous trends among administrators dispersed among the ethnic groups. A few would end up in the Sluzhba navy. *Very strange*, she thought, *after their years of training deep in the heart of snowy Russia.* A very few received notes that said only that their assignments were "open." 75 was one of them.

A clerk took 75 aside and told her that she would be assigned to a Moscow training site and to English language training. She received written orders and a copy of the review of her academic and military performance a few days later in a heavy thick envelope. She and the captain had said their goodbyes the night before his departure for an exercise on the Pacific coast. The system had let the captain climb just so far. 75 had grabbed the system by its throat and manipulated it for her benefit. They both knew this, and they left unuttered the awareness that they would never see each other again. Neither would miss the other.

SHE WAS RELIEVED by her assignment to the English-speaking cadre. She had never liked the Rumanians and Japanese, who thronged to her father's lectures for visiting dignitaries during the tourist months. She had asked her father why they were different from her fellow students and their Sunday guests. "They simply are. No one really knows why." She feared being assigned to the Chinese, Korean, or Japanese cadre. They didn't smell right, and she disliked their crowded trains, pollution, and food. But why English? She read technical English from computer manuals, but she had not heard a spoken word of American or British English except in movies, which she presumed did not teach her the English she would encounter on the streets of London or New York. Or Brisbane or Toronto for that matter. "How would I fare in New York" she asked 4? "You will be an *otlichnika*, an outstanding servant of the state wherever you land." They both knew the English curriculum included far more than just language, and the tradecraft curriculum extended well beyond books and classes. *There will be rewards.*

Just before the classroom phase of her training at Yasenevo ended, during a lecture on the British and American stock markets, two guards entered the classroom and put a black hood over her head. They dragged her down the corridor to a small covered truck with no windows and threw her in the back. There were no seats or benches. 75 removed the hood and saw nothing but the dirty wooden walls. She counted the minutes, about sixty, until the truck slowed and turned left onto a bumpy dirt road. Pain set in, and she braced herself against the wall on the driver's side, assuming he would avoid going over pot holes that would hurt himself. After the third hour, the truck stopped and the back door opened. "Ne dalshe. (This is as far as you go.)" The driver threw her a heavy winter coat, got back into the front, and drove off.

SHE WAS AS disoriented as the driver had meant her to be. Given how long the truck had traveled and allowing for error caused by the bumps and pain, she calculated she was no more than a hundred and twenty-five kilometers from the classroom. She needed shelter and water. She could go without food for three days, but a sleet storm in the next few hours could kill her.

A dim shadow in the distance appeared to be a barn, and she stumbled toward it as quickly as her bruised body allowed. Reciting I will beat the bastards to herself, she pulled herself with each step from the muck that sucked her feet down. She closed on the barn and opened a side door. She fell on a pile of hay, covered herself with it, and tried to gain some warmth.

She awoke after dark. A large, grizzled peasant stood over her. Many of the old men who fought in the Great War still spoke the dialects of the villages from which they had been yanked to serve as human mine clearers for Zhukov's tanks. They had stayed where they were at war's end, and as the decades passed, fallen into old age. They were ignorant of politics and the Afghan war. They knew nothing but sunrise, sunset, meager harvests, and the mud of old Russia. 75 hoped he spoke a language she understood. He asked, "*Ktor vwee* (who are you)?" She said she had gotten a ride in a truck and been let off when the driver turned south. She was en route to visit her family. The old farmer grinned and lurched toward her. As he extended his arms toward her waist, she broke his nose with a right-hand chop. Blood gushed from the mangled cartilage onto his smock.

His old wife entered, looked at the flowing blood, and without comment invited 75 into her warm kitchen for a meal. 75 swallowed her soup in gulps and finished a plate of potatoes and cabbage with her fingers. The old woman handed her a heavy blanket and led her across the line of blood drops to a straw-filled stall in the barn, one far from the door and the wind.

The sun had risen when 75 got up. She scratched at the indentions the straw had left on her face and headed for the kitchen. The peasant woman shuffled to the stove and ladled a plate of kasha for her. After 75 had eaten, the woman inspected her face and hands for cuts and bruises, then gave her two eggs and a large piece of dark bread wrapped in a shawl. At the door, she pointed across the muddy field toward the road and said, "*Derevna* (the village)." 75 thanked her, smiled, and left.

She found the village and its tavern. Huddled against the almost-hidden wall of a tractor shed, she waited for a smallish man to leave the bar. When one finally staggered though the door, he tripped over the leg she extended. 75 removed her shoes and, with them, the GPS. She put the man's boots on and recovered his naked feet with her own gym shoes. "That should hold the bastards for a few hours," she whispered and, "God help you" to the man, frost already forming on his frame. 75 broke the lock on the shed's office and slept until after sunset. When she left, she saw his footprints leading to the locked office and away again. She hoped it did not rain before he made it to wherever he was going.

75, cold and filthy, stood by the road. The snow was melting, and the spatter from passing cars speckled her. The pock marked driver of a large oil tanker picked her up. He and his cab smelled even worse than she did. After they had traveled an hour or so, they neared Moscow. She got off when the driver stopped to eat and got another ride in a minivan filled with drugged musicians who looked her over and invited their new friend to join them at their next gig. She declined. When she saw signs for a familiar suburb, she left them.

After walking for much of the afternoon, she glimpsed tall buildings in the growing gloom, then a plowed field, a fenced compound, and finally, the double gate. A sergeant took her picture, sent it to the school's security office, and let her through. A package lay on 75's pillow. New clothes and a message. "We drove a hundred-twenty-five kilometers to pick up the GPS. The little man was unhappy. A second system had been sewn into the collar of your heavy coat. Better luck next time."

A FEW DAYS after 75's return, 41 asked, "That was a tough exercise. Why do you take all this shit from these dolts?"

"They're not dolts. They do what they do because it's their job. They have passed the point of creativity or greater competence. Most of them have blundered somewhere along the line, and no department head wants them."

41 shuffled ahead. "You are so smart. Could you not find a more profitable way of earning a living, like working for one of the new billionaires or, even better, becoming one yourself?"

"I know exactly where I would be if I had kept my old job, if I stayed with it for forty years in a small room with eight or ten people, some of whom didn't bathe frequently. I don't want to know the future in specific terms. My father and his friends will die. I need a replacement—where, who, or what I do not care. It is a something I cannot define.

"I'm like my grandmother the sniper. No routines, just good things and bad things happening randomly. My father told his students that they must do their best work in their twenties and thirties. Afterwards they might fall prey to *Poshlost*, you know, that combination of sloppiness, lack of ambition, and mindless satisfaction with what you possess. Remember one inescapable fact, 41, Russia was here a thousand years ago, and it will be here a thousand years from now. Every nation in the world will try to smuggle people, oil, diamonds, and money into and out of Russia. I don't like the uniforms here, but they look better than the rags of my former colleagues. The food is better here, too, and I like you, 41 As for billionaires and millionaires, they fall from grace with the political winds, and some of them get killed in very unpleasant ways."

75 HAD SEEN DEATH and caused it, just like Grandmother Sniper. She felt neither exhilaration nor despair at her current status, but she did see herself as having risen above the rabble. No dirty dishes on her champagne table. Her father had succeeded not because of his connections but because his labors made singular contributions to ballistic missilery and submarine launching systems. She wanted to gain power on her merits just as he had. At Yasenevo, she concluded that she was getting close to something.

This is a new time, she thought. *Who cares about dull authors like Leskov or Herzen and other so-called reformers of a bygone century?* Her schoolmasters had to preach the virtues of those incomprehensible authors now that they were on the official curriculum in some of the universities. Why they had to teach their dim understanding of Russia before 1917 was incomprehensible to her. Her modern Sluzhba school was one of those that provided entry to the burgeoning middle class and sometimes to wealth, even though it bore no similarity to her university. Surviving this training was a ticket into the nomenclatura she wanted, even if one had to eliminate a few low lifes and finger a few who were unworthy of her new life. After all the nonsense was peeled away, her courses portrayed Russia as a world power ever enlarging its strategic interests, whatever western newspapers and their simpering journalists wrote. 75 saw a glimmer of interest there.

CHAPTER 11

English House

THE ENGLISH-SPEAKING group gave up their awkward uniforms and exercise clothes to the ancient clerk who hobbled around his little kingdom in slippers like a Chekhovian grand uncle. 75 and her mates were allowed to take nothing but the clothes they wore. A few smuggled cherished tools or pens in their underwear next to their skin. They climbed into two buses with decent springs. None spoke.

The buses headed to Moscow's outskirts and disgorged their passengers outside a shaded brick house with green shutters. It lay in ten hectares of tree-spotted lawns and gardens. The front of the house had a red door with a handsome brass knocker and a bell on the right side of the door frame. Even 41 was moved from her stolidity.

"75, why all this? Is this to prepare us for jobs in the Second Directorate reading newspapers?" 41 went to a bathroom and shouted, "this is too much. Why do you need all this equipment to take a shit?" 75 looked around and replied that she thought the decorations and gadgets were mostly unnecessary but that the heat might be welcome in winter.

75 WAS NOW Mary Ellen Hughes, and 41 had become Shirley Woodman. 34 was now Frank O'Toole and 12, Al Barnes. They lived in a small house at the back of the property. The buses' other passengers were distributed among a few other houses, some bigger, a few smaller. The main house was painted white with dark red trim. Its portico reached out over the white gravel drive and the newish Ford SUV sitting there. The floors were polished with an American wax whose perfume barely covered the leafy odor that permeated the rest of the compound. The carpets were expensive, but bad reproductions of bad paintings hung on the walls. There was a swimming pool in the garden, a TV in each bedroom, and every imaginable appliance in the kitchen. The bathroom soaps and shampoos were gentle. Mary Ellen was assigned a college girl's bedroom with posters of rock and film stars. She loathed it. She had seen American movies, but this room was reality.

They learned how to do the chores of an American middle-class homeowner for themselves. "My God how can they live like this," she muttered to herself. How can you paint a picture, perform espionage work, blow up a bridge, or formulate algorithms if you have to patch plumbing, fix the roof, and shovel out a driveway—to say nothing of painting the backyard furniture. They learned basic car maintenance as well. Her father never needed to do these things, neither at his flat or at the dacha. Grandma sniper and her friends saved the country, my father and his colleagues made Russia a great nation, and I am stepping off into a new abyss. She looked around the room with its terrifying, yet mesmerizing, colors and shapes. *Before this, I knew what I knew. Now I don't know certainty or ignorance or the difference between them.*

Her bathroom had mirrors and fluffy towels and its own seductive smells. She changed her simple trainers for a young American woman's underwear, sweater, and skirt. They smelled clean, and that changed her mood. But only a little.

Most of the eight men and four women spoke little English, and each of the hundreds of items inside and outside the house had labels with the Russian name and its most-used American name. American and British music played constantly, and a series of instructors with different accents and perfect grammar gave each student three separate hours of instruction for five days a week. Each student got a smattering of all the accents in order to make accurate identifications of those they would meet. The English language movies continued. Mary Ellen liked Bogart, Gable, and Gielgud.

ON HER FIRST DAY at English House, she lingered in her large tiled bathroom. She turned the shower handle on and off. Hot, warm, and cold. Solid stream and soft. She had never seen anything dedicated to whim rather than necessity. But the immersion training in this upwardly mobile American house had its effects. The men discarded their military walk, put their hands in their pockets, and learned to speak with each other informally. Military haircuts disappeared.

Schoolchildren's backpacks lay in a pile at the front door. The twelve found the study of grammar-school curricula an intrusion, but in the end, amusing. Shirley, when she married, wanted her children brought up in the ways of Springfield, Massachusetts rather than Tomsk. In Springfield, misbehaving children there were corrected with a smile and kind words instead of a slap across the face. The four women were encouraged to carry pocketbooks and fix their makeup as needed. No shiny noses at English House.

Mary Ellen Hughes's principal language tutor, Roman A., had served as commercial attaché in Washington and had a lively family familiar with American gadgets: electric can openers, various kinds of coffee pots, steel-clad aluminum pans, a microwave, cookbooks, and contraptions that Mary Ellen could not figure out. He taught with no enthusiasm.

Unlike Yasenevo, English House seethed with tranquility. No one barked at her during class to muster outside immediately and run five kilometers through a muddy field. One day, an instructor entered the kitchen and told her to make a three-egg ham and cheese omelet. She grabbed the cookbook above the gas stove, read the instructions, and went to work. The instructor howled it was the worst he had ever eaten. Though one from a truck stop outside Mobile, Alabama was almost as bad, he admitted. "We know you can blow up warehouses. We have yet to learn if you can live like a well-traveled English speaker." He left the dining room with a sour look.

CHAPTER 12

Krushkin

ANOTHER BROWN ENVELOPE lay on her bed. She put the odds at 50-50 that the contents originated from Him. Although He had no formal title, He was the chief of deep-cover ops in English-speaking countries. The note ordered her to wait at her new home's front door for a car and driver who would arrive at 10:30 am and deliver her to . . . street, where she would await further instructions. She dressed in her new American clothes and wondered what impression they would make on Him.

The car arrived, drove to the Center of town, and deposited her at a dowdy building with a plaque that read DEUTCHE ALUMINIUM GMBH. She entered, gave the name Maria Helena, and was directed to an office on the third floor, where an armed guard instructed her to sit on a wooden bench. She was sure that no one in her class had ever seen Him, the faceless legend. To meet Him was a high honor. Few alive had enjoyed his company. He was said to have run the operation that captured a truck load of American Stinger missiles in Afghanistan and saved a Russian tank column from ambush as it left the country. He was not in the pictured hierarchy, and no one seemed to know if he had ever been assigned to an English-speaking country.

IGNATS ALEXANDRAVITCH KRUSHKIN and her father shared a past, Katya was sure. When she entered his office, a voice erupted from behind a beautiful and oddly feminine desk, probably from Tsarist times. "And how are you today, Katerina Mikhailovna? I understand that you have done very well in our very demanding courses. Are you as smart as your father? Probably not. Few people are." He spoke intimately as if he were a seldom seen relative visiting for a few days.

Krushkin had full cheeks and scanty eyebrows. The eyes between them almost bulged with inquiry. He had always wanted to know. His gaze captured exuberance, satisfaction, and menace all at once. His chest was huge, belly concealed below the desktop. He leaned forward over his desk and gave the impression of one who always wanted to know something from his guest.

Krushkin did not rise or shake hands but greeted her with a voice and accent that would have done credit to the Alexandrinski Theater. His language was not that of the Muscovite bureaucrat but a Petersburg poet. He behaved as though she, her parents, and her entire family were old friends. Because he did not rise for guests, he was rumored to have very short legs. He had a shaved head, and his ear lobes drooped almost to his collar. His mismatched shirt and tie did not come from Nevski Prospect or London. Probably New York. They were just shy of being gaudy. Krushkin, Katerina thought, should have a job teaching and reading Akmatova and Pushkin instead of managing the twenty or thirty men and women he had sent out into the world. Some of them never came back.

As soon as Katerina had settled into a nineteenth-century French chair, Krushkin began. "I am of two minds about asking you to join us in this special section of the Sluzhba. You are clever, but Russia likes brilliant older people, not smart young ones. That is why the oligarchs have such trouble. One or two of them died from over achievement. One poor fellow took a long time to die painfully. Still, I have asked you to see me because I have an offer. Until yesterday, I had two offers. The first involved working with an experienced case officer on a very profitable target. He was a very experienced officer who had great successes over the years. Perhaps he was burned out and I didn't see it. An Australian constable caught him exiting a closed facility. He jumped from the second story and ran. He should never have run. The constable chased him and shot him dead."

He stopped as though waiting for the effect of his measured sentences to sink in. "We believe you have the right skills for a mission of unusual importance to us and possible death for you. You will work alone. If you follow our profession's detailed rules and inform their use with your acute intelligence, you will succeed. Hanssen lasted twenty years. The likes of Philby and Burgess and MacLean will never be seen again. They followed the rules of our game until they had played the game too long.

"There is a splendid word in our language, *dostachno*, (enough). Don't push matters beyond their natural boundaries. When you have spent time in the field, you will see what I mean. This is a dangerous career. This section has had a disappointing year. One couple were killed, dismembered, and thrown into the Mogadishu River. Another agent was murdered in a bar fight in Bangkok. Another was run over in Las Vegas. Kindly policemen caught a few and, in due course, we will make an exchange. Meantime, they live poorly in unpleasant jails. The opposition grows smarter every year. Much has changed since the days of Ames and Hanssen, who were successful not because they were proficient, but because the Americans weren't very clever.

"Your mission will take place mainly in America. If you accept, you will work alone against sophisticated opposition with no support to speak of—no help from the residentura in Washington and not much from the Center here. Parts of the mission will be pleasant, especially for a woman like you. Others maybe not so. All your skills will come into play. Your nerves will be severely tested, as when swimming away from the drunken Dagestani. Your judgment of people will get you imprisoned, dead, or a medal on the wall of the First Directorate.

"By the way, you had keen insight into 6. We concluded that you are good at discerning fair from foul. We all agreed he could never serve.

"First, I wish to give you something of a gift with strings. It is a going away present, a subject for study here and a reward for you when you return." Jilly had never heard of Krushkin's generosity toward his juniors. "Go to that table and bring me that one meter by two meter folio." Katya obeyed. "You have heard of Norman Rockwell the American painter? This a first folio of his early and war time work signed by him. You will learn more from these pages than from most books. He knew his country and loved it, as I do mine." Krushkin flipped through the pages, stopping at those he especially liked. It's a shame we had to acquire it as we did. We had a man in New York who turned sour. He couldn't be left free to gossip with his fellow gallery owners. He visited the afterworld sooner than he might have otherwise. My operative covered the death by stealing that folio in order to make appear a murder. He passed it to one of us on a beach in Brooklyn, someone who put it in the Consulate General's pouch for me. I love it, but if you return to this office with a crown on your head you may have it. Study it before you go and put it your locker.

"I propose a mission for you in America where you will live as an ambitious young business woman. The usual risks of being identified and suborned or killed by a foreign service will be with you forever. You will live well as a very comfortable American. You need not like them, but I doubt that you will dislike them. You must not marry or have children. Relationships, except in the line of duty, would be dangerous.

"Oddly, your success will go unnoticed by the Americans. You and we will know when and if you have succeeded. The Americans will never be the wiser. You will understand that later. After you have completed this mission, you can either accept a new assignment abroad or come back. You may not correspond with or see your beloved father for the duration of your stay in America. Neither your father nor your classmates know of our meeting. I cannot tell you more. Before proceeding, we will want to see how you get along with Americans, how you socialize with them, how you speak with them, and how you might live with them. Could you not tell me tomorrow morning if you accept my offer? A car will pick you up at 10:30."

She found herself wandering from Kruskin's words and said: "Those are splendid tapestries."

"Yes, they are. One of our colleagues passed himself off as a dealer, and when his mission was complete, he returned here. Somehow a few of his goods ended up in our office rather than in a museum or in our warehouse, where few would see them." *And he probably kept a few for his dacha in the South,* she thought. She noticed that the figure of God appeared in two of the tapestries. *Did He have a secret life?*

Katerina was confused as much by the offer as by Krushkin's beautiful language. He was dark and expressive, and his origins were impossible to fathom. His presence and conversation might better have brightened the professors' lounge at Petersburg

University. He lacked the pallor that marred the facial bones of Northern Russians. His bright shirt and colored tie were all of a piece with his consumption of cups of tea drunk from Belleek, the pot refilled every few hours without his asking. He arrived from the Kremlin gates at Aluminium GMBH at eight in the morning in a chauffeur-driven civilian car chosen randomly from the Sluzhba garage. He returned promptly to the Kremlin at six in the evening. He was not thought to be married. Katerina mused that every man had a smidgeon of corruption in him, but she could not identify Krushkin's. Someone bought him his New York shirts. He was a loyal servant of the state, whatever guise it happened to inhabit. "Tomorrow, Katya?"

"Yes, tomorrow."

ON THE WAY back to English House, she congratulated herself. Abroad and alone, she would not work for a demanding resident who could wake her at any hour for an emergency. Recruiting drunks and addicts at the UN was out. No security agents would hobble her office life or her social initiatives. No one would report her for an unlocked safe or shortage of embassy stationery. No one would tell her where to live or what color curtains to hang.

Undercover as a civilian in an English-speaking country meant freedom from the gossip, surveillance, and heavy-handed guidance that those on their first foreign tour had to bear if they worked in an embassy or consulate. If the FBI or MI5 caught her, five or six years in a dingy jail could pass before she was exchanged. If another country's service found her interfering with their missions, they could kill her with no one the wiser.

Living away from her father, his apartment, and his homey dacha would be lonely in mind and soul. Staying overseas doubled the pain. Would she ever find someone as close to her as he? Nobody or no place else could fill that void. And then, too, he would not be there to push her up the ranks or get her sent to a desirable post after her apprenticeship. Or perhaps help mitigate a youthful blunder.

Like a clever salesman, Krushkin had failed to disclose the bits and pieces that bedeviled operators abroad. As an unmarried single officer with no web of connections in the First Directorate, her future would depend largely on the persons at the Center who read her reports. They would likely argue to Krushkin to send her instructions above and beyond her immediate set of orders. These would usually be off the point of her mission and awkward in their superfluous directions. The Center's readers sometimes developed an animus toward those fortunate enough to obtain a post abroad with no nearby boss. The mediocre who had not worked in the field and who had little hope of advancement tended to envy colleagues who led more glamorous lives. Many delighted in the alleged sins of others and in complicating their work.

THE CAR PICKED her up the next morning. Krushkin looked up as she sat in the same chair she had the day before. She gave him no time for pleasantries. "I have decided yes."

"I thought you would. Make no mistake, we do understand that your principle motive is not service. You want to be sponsored and funded by the state. You want a life of the mind that neither your instructors nor your tests could define. You want to work outside the boundaries of our ancient culture. Don't stray too far. Produce good work and keep us all out of trouble. I do not wish to see your alias name above the fold in the *New York Times*."

Katya twitched in her chair. Krushkin reminded her of Jupiter declaiming from on high in a painting she had admired at The Hermitage. The previous day's collegial tone had disappeared. The elegant language continued, but the sugared words were missing. He evinced no wit, charm, or friendliness, only the brusk language of a field commander ordering his men to advance.

Every country has a Krushkin, whom the people below fear and whom those above need. All that varied were the local colors and flavors. In Krushkin's case, they involved hating the oligarchs, loving the near-mythic Russian past, preferring New York shirts and ties, and treasuring any harm he could effect on Russia's enemies. "Remember one more thing, Katya. Politicians come and go. We keep the world in balance."

"HERE IS YOUR mission. A Harvard professor named Ingraham knows much about germs. So do his competitors and colleagues. So do we. We know enough from hacking into his computer that he knows almost how to box them with a long half-life in a safely sealed container anywhere beneath the ground or sea. He came upon this knowledge by accident, what the French call *bricolage*---tinkering. Neither we nor he knows how to disperse the contents of this germ bomb remotely, securely, and at our bidding. We and the West are close to fabricating a fuse. The communications link to the fuse poses difficulties. He is getting close to a solution of packaging, preserving, igniting, and dispersal. On that score, we, alas, are a bit behind. Disaster would follow if the professor achieved a solution before us. My masters would rain hell on me and possibly take away one of my dachas.

"We will soon be at war with the Chechens. Sooner than many of my colleagues think. They have no outlet to the sea and cause mischief at their borders. They don't mind blowing up theaters either. Our leader with the unattractive birthmarks has many enemies, some very close in belief to his wife. He may get his retirement dacha in the South before he wants. Before that happens, I want you to scoop out Professor Ingraham's brain and send it to us. We believe he has two vulnerabilities: young ladies of high intelligence and pride in his work. You have an easy way in. He thinks he know a lot about art and visits museums in Boston.

"Our branch chief and his assistants will educate you in the ways of your new environment. Your time spent at the Hermitage should stand you in good stead. Do not get me in trouble, Katya. I want you to have two dachas, one at Sochi, where you like the environs, and one in snow country north of Moscow. Remember we had failures this year. I want success from you that I can trumpet at a Kremlin dinner.

"One thing we do well here. We define people. We asked your father, who is brilliant and who works well with very clever men, if you were superior to the rest. He answered in the affirmative. We have a meritocracy, whatever contrary views others hold, and you have entered it. You have been given a very difficult and potentially dangerous mission. You will be on your own, as they say in the West. I am sending you abroad into a pack of wolves. You will have no mentor but yourself.

"Did you ever read a journal by Olearius, who traveled Russia from north to south in the early seventeenth century? He came from the West, as we knew it then. He was a very keen observer of our country, of its faults and strengths. In the end he knew more about Russia than all but a few Russians. You will go from the East to the West and tell us amazing things about America and how far they must come to catch up to us."

Krushkin, now the professor guiding a student, leaned forward and spoke softly as from deep wisdom. "A Frenchman named de Toqueville wrote an excellent book on the early American republic. He traveled in every level of society in all the states and at the end of his wanderings knew more about America than the Americans. His predictions about its future were surprisingly accurate. Few read him. An English translation of his work gathers dust on the top shelf of the book shelf in your dining room. When you return from America I expect you to know as much about America in this age as that Frenchman knew about it in his."

THE THEFT OF SCIENTIFIC accomplishment was the kernel of Katya's mission. No dangerous containers of radioactive materiel or canisters of a new gun powder were needed. The fruit of the professor's work could be sent back to the Center on a few thumb drives. According to the analysts at the Center, her work would be unique. A team of scientists would examine data she stole. They would let her know promptly if the material had been bogus or useful and tell her which of Professor Ingraham's associates seemed worth hacking. She had vulnerabilities. A busybody might spend time and money to discover that her origins were fake, or a generic search might get hold of her drives before she passed them to her drop.

Katya had conceived of her life as a journey to who knew where, an unstructured trip ending with a dacha at Sochi where she could write her memoirs. But leaving His office, she changed her mind. Her life, she realized, was theater. Her father was her agent, Krushkin the demanding director, she the female lead, and the not-yet-known Professor Ingraham the male lead, the hero, the faux man of action who made things happen. Or so he thought. The crowd that hired her for her role were the permanent audience who would write reviews and forbid or permit the play to open the second night.

"MARY ELLEN, dinner for four tonight! The others will play bridge and would like some snacks. Pick a decent white wine for the fish." The Chief smiled as he gave the orders. He had been stationed at the San Francisco consulate, where had made the acquaintance of the Italian fishermen. They brought him their best catches, or so they told him. The FBI blew his cover at an ill-sited dead drop, and though he could not work abroad again, he was content showing off his knowledge at English House, where his students were bright and enthusiastic. He dressed in the Brooks Brothers clothes he had retained from his tour. Mary Ellen saw a properly tied bow tie for the first time.

The weeks went on. Her group of four yelled and screamed at each other in English until someone slipped and ranted in Russian. The loser always had to make dinner. Mary Ellen learned to moan and groan in English, useful, for she was made to suffer extensive dental work. The dentist had practiced in the Bronx and used only American materials and techniques. One cavity was left so a Danish dentist could document her visit. A brusque surgeon removed tonsils and appendix against the worry that a visit to an American hospital might spark a close look at her medical records. Her new medical records were sent to a Danish clinic, where they would be held like any other European citizen's.

Mary Ellen changed tires, mowed the lawn, trimmed the hedges, read fashion magazines, and newspapers and sports pages that covered New England. She built football, baseball, and hockey vocabularies. She learned the names of the Canadian teams and their stars from her cover home town. She practiced parking and tolerated the tedium of waiting in line for a driver's license. She learned to cook lobster and fish. She used American computers and studied American accounting techniques. She recoiled from her instruction one afternoon. "Chief, do Americans still use double-entry book keeping?"

HER PRIVATE INSTRUCTOR from the Makarov Institute, Pavel Ivanovich, focused on English in the context of all things naval and wove nautical terms into their informal evening lessons. At their first meeting, he gave her a marked up copy of *Knight's Modern Seamanship*. "There is mechanical information here and some wisdom. The sea is a wondrous place, dangerous sometimes, but very seductive when you get to know it. Did you know that there are six names for different ocean bottoms?" *Pushkin and Akhmatova did not write very much about the sea*, she thought.

MARY ELLEN often signed out at the guard post often to visit her new family. She felt like a freed galley slave when she entered the warmth of the Ivanovich house. Pavel was short, dumpy, and fighting a losing battle against middle-aged girth. He wore overused carpet slippers and the shards of an undress naval uniform that had seen too many wearings on too many wet and snowy Arctic nights, His shirt retained its collar, but no buttons or rank. He was shaven, had combed hair, and the opposite in every way of the starched instructors at Yasenevo.

His eyes always lit up when he saw Mary Ellen's face at the door. He guided her to a comfortable old chair, all the while welcoming her as a guest, delighted to be introducing this particular student to the variations of the sea. Beside her on a stand was a small dish of *zakuskie* from his own garden and a tiny ceremonial glass of chilled vodka. He retreated to his own chair and sat there the whole evening, benign and comfortable. He seemed more to bless Katya than to instruct her. Rather than just giving her a new language, he changed her attitudes toward the ocean, foreign travel, and western ways of doing business. Somehow, he also imbued her with the ability to make the calm responses needed to live with a family that included a child.

ONE EVENING AFTER DINNER, long after Mary Ellen had come to think of Pavel's study as the most delightful and satisfying classroom she had ever encountered, he leaned back, sipped his vodka, and sighed regretfully. "I have brought you as far as I can on dry land. Your sailing instructor will teach you more." All had somehow divined that this was this was her last visit. While Pavel's wife prepared a celebratory meal with delicacies almost like Katerina's father had served at his Sunday lunches, Pavel and Mary Ellen played a game. Pavel would say a naval word or expression, and Mary Ellen would define it. After one hundred and three correct answers, she could not define neap tide. They all laughed, Pavel rose, patted her shoulder, and gave her a passing grade on his spontaneous examination. They sat to eat. At the end, all three walked to the door without words. Mary Ellen handed Pavel his worn book almost as a gift. He accepted reluctantly. They kissed three times in the Old Church manner and said goodbye, not *Poka* (until we meet). Mary Ellen looked back and saw them at a window. A decent side to her career existed after all.

THE CHIEF SOUGHT her out after breakfast. Mary Ellen removed the rubber gloves she used when scouring pots and pans and walked down the hall to his office. The lion's-head door handle came from Rome, the door from a Los Angeles antique shop. He perched on his American desk chair, cheek bones in the air, and locked Mary Ellen in the eye. Like a stern but solicitous headmaster, he folded his hands in an almost prayerful position and began. "We are about to spread your wings. We think that you are almost ready to go abroad on a short trip to Germany. You will use your permanent working alias, Jillian Augusta Carlson. That is the only name you will use on your journeys in Europe and America. You will be a traveling American from a prosperous family who has become Germanized and had too much money lavished on her."

"I have never been spoiled, Chief."

"There are other votes around here on that subject, Mary Ellen. Your tests show you speak a very serviceable, if not elegant, German of Berlin. We want you to leave a credible paper trail of a life in Europe. You will have a native German-speaking friend accompanying you. You will meet her in a Copenhagen bar and discover you have similar tastes in art. You will tour the museums, churches, and scenery, especially in the south. You will develop a liking, perhaps a love, for the Baroque. The Hermitage is not strong there. You will have dinner at my favorite restaurant in Hagenau.

"The woman you will be traveling with is native German, a university graduate, and more knowledgeable about the country than any guide book. She will report to us on your demeanor, your speech, and how you handle the ups and downs. You seem, even by our standards, to display a less than normal sense of humor. I do not want to read in the *Frankfurter Zeitung* that a mysterious American woman has maimed two bouncers outside a strip club. Understood? The impromptu is not for beginners"

"Yes, Chief."

"Your new name is . . .

"See you in a month."

HER NEW NAME had been taken from a child killed with her entire family in a car accident twenty-five years earlier in a North Dakota county whose records had burned. The dead child had moved across the border into Canada, where her prosperous grandparents raised here and left her a decent inheritance.

Mary Ellen returned to her room and found an already-stamped US passport for Jillian Augusta Carlson, a Danish driver's license, credit cards, pictures of her grandparents, and a tourist's sample of clothes with German and Danish labels. Two pairs of German shoes sat on the floor. A bag of European cosmetics confused her with their non-American names. Very different, she thought in English, from the twenty-five kilo rucksack I had to carry on the last exercises.

CHAPTER 13

Lars

As THOUGH she had been lifted to the heavens, Jilly left English House the next day. Unknown hands spirited away her clothes and baggage, and a fishing trawler picked her up at a desolate pier and transferred her to a Danish motor yacht. On the way, she became Jillian Augusta Carlson, who had entered Demark from Germany as a tourist on an EU passport. After entering the Kattegat, Jilly sailed into a small harbor on Denmark's east coast where she would enter Copenhagen with her minder in order acquire the skills needed to handle a forty-foot sailboat by herself in rough waters. The skipper of the boat that brought her from a rotting wooden pier to the open sea said nothing to Jillian, and she stayed silent the whole trip.

Helga Bauer, who would be her escort for the next months, met her at the dock and gave her a Danish sweater. She examined her newest pupil with a mask of polite acceptance that concealed a sergeant's skepticism of new troopers. She would be, however, Katya's only true and adult friend since she had left home. 69 and a few others would be honest and competent operators, she could trust them in the field, but they never touched her Russian conscience, the impalpable substance that told you what was right and what was wrong in that vast unwritten code of Russian behavior.

Helga spoke native German, English, and yachtsmen's Danish. "Welcome to the new Germany, the union of the Marshall Plan West and the Stalinist East. It works pretty well. How was the trip? You will be at sea quite a bit from now on. I hope you don't get seasick."

"Thanks for the sweater; you got the size right."

"I have booked us into a small hotel, clean but noisy. The stairs creak. No cameras at the front desk or in the hallways. Willy, the owner, is an acquaintance. He's used to tourists and yachtsmen coming and going. Be careful with him. He likes girls more than boys, but he takes no for an answer."

"What is the next step? Do we play it by ear, or do you have an itinerary?"

"First, you will descend to breakfast tomorrow morning like the moderately spoiled child of prosperous parents who left you cash enough to wander around Europe until the thrill wore off. A little bit of swagger! You will receive looks from the men, but do not return them. The morning coffee at Willy's is black and strong. Drink it as though you are used to it and like it.

"We would like you to pick up enough Danish to show your worldliness and ability to adapt to a different society. Shouldn't be too difficult. I understand you have a gift for languages. Later, we will travel all over Germany by car. Tomorrow morning, you will meet Lars. Tomorrow afternoon, we will drive by the Computer Institute where you will be said to have studied. We will find a catalogue so that you can speak meaningfully about the courses you never took there.

"You will like Lars, your sailing instructor. He is much older than you. He has no education and rough manners. All he knows about you is that you have a whim to learn to sail. He's been around the Kattegat for years. I'm surprised he doesn't have an island named after him." Helga turned serious. "Your goal with Lars is to acquire a high state of competency in tranquil waters. The Kattegat will be your pond. It has hundreds of little islands, and you will almost never be out of sight of one. The wind here is gentle and comes mostly from the west. It's a good place to learn sailing."

"I have never sailed."

"Just act as though you love the water and have always wanted to learn. By the way, I understand that you have a cavity to be filled. We will attend to that before you leave. If it starts to hurt, tell me."

Jilly and her new friend drove into the city and meandered through the side streets toward the waterfront, where they sauntered around the docks. They stopped at a two-masted boat with the name *Reichenbach* painted in black letters on the stern. A lean man surveyed his visitors. *The dark one has good legs and the tight T-shirt does her no harm. Jacobsson did well for me this time.*

"Hi, Helga You must be Jillian Carlson. I understand you want to sail. You could not have picked a better boat or a finer instructor."

LARS JENSEN was a man of the Baltic. He was conceived in the back room of a bar in Riga and born in the galley of a British fishing trawler. At fourteen, he had shipped out on a freighter that sailed to Buenos Aires and back. He killed his first man in Sao Paulo and earned a seaman's book on derelict ships under unlicensed captains. When out of work or tired of sleeping in stinking bunks under the turbines, he stayed ashore and gambled. Too good at cards, he twice found himself unconscious in the alleys of Göteborg, He was young and strong, and he recovered easily and well from the vicissitudes of his unusual existence. Along the way, he picked up the German, Swedish, and Danish of the ports. When he saw the American trade pick up, he learned English.

"Please call me Lars, Jillian. We will have a good time." Lars Jensen was not his true name. After he had killed two men in a Göteborg brawl, he fled, pleading with a trawler captain to take him to Copenhagen. The captain took Lars' last Euros and stashed him under the propeller shaft. That was the last time he used his seaman's book.

In Denmark, a Sluzhba stringer who happened on him in a bar saw poverty, despair, and intelligence. The next morning, Lars awoke in a dingy room. In it was one Herr Jacobson. Jacobsson sat in the only chair. "If you like your present life, my friend, stay in this miserable room. If you would like a more settled and prosperous future, come downstairs and we will talk."

Jacobsson waited at a table set with two large breakfasts. Lars came down, ate, and listened. Some days later, he got his new name, papers that identified him as a Danish citizen, a haircut, and civilian clothes. In return, he would perform tasks that his new mater Herr Jacobsson assigned. He agreed to abstain from violence lest his old name and present finger prints turn up on lists of wanted felons.

The furrows of a hard life disappeared from his face. After a few courier jobs for Jacobsson, he found a ketch he liked and bought it with money from his benefactor. He learned enough tourists' English to take a few Americans around the islands off Copenhagen and became part of the community that picked up scanty livings along the Baltic shore. Jacobsson kept the seaman's book.

"IT IS GOOD to meet you, Lars."

"Let us started right away. Please get in the boat. We will have an introduction to sailing." Lars grabbed Jilly's hand, and she jumped clumsily onto the boat's deck. The tide was low, and the jump nearly two feet. She looked him over. *Sleazy and corrupt but probably good at his job. Unmarried and bored with women after whoring around for twenty-five years. Calloused hands and strong wrists, high cheek bones like an aristocratic Swede. I wonder if he knows his parents.*

"First thing, put on your red life jacket. It's the law. It is also common sense. It has two red flares, which you will never need. These waters are usually calm, but if you fall overboard, we want to know where you are. In the Kattegat, it is almost impossible to be pitched out of a boat without an island in sight."

In the beginning, Jillian spent three hours a day sailing, but that became four or five as she grew to like Lars and the Baltic's gentle behavior. Lars never criticized and made corrections gently. *No pushups after mistakes?*

"Sailing is easy, Jillian. Casting off, tying up, and storms are tricky. You cannot defeat the sea and the sea cannot defeat you. You must always watch and compromise. Have you noticed that no one laughs at the sea, but the sea gives you a deep quiet if you bring the right attitude to it."

In its drive toward the ocean, Moscow had almost obliterated the old ironwork fixtures fitted into the wharves of the rivers that ran into the Baltic. Cranes, tracks, and huge mooring devices replaced the beautiful handmade bits and bollards of the eighteenth and nineteenth centuries. At that cost, Saint Petersburg harbor became the Center of Baltic trade. Not so Copenhagen, whose harbor masters had preserved the massive iron fittings to which the largest sail boat could tie up. Lars used them with pride.

Helga came frequently to Lars's dock with a lunch basket that gave her unrestricted entry. When Lars found wind he liked, he opened his thermos and poured them all coffee. They would sit back, smelling it and the salt and congratulating themselves on their good fortune and health. One day, Jilly asked Lars why he had named his boat *Reichenbach*.

"I saw the name in a book once. It seemed aristocratic. Do you know, I have picked up business from Americans and British who recognize it? I don't know why." Helga smiled, glancing at the large quantities of splendid food she had brought: paté, French bread, and small pieces of marinated meat. Lars inspected it as though he had never seen such extravagance. As they pulled ashore to picnic on an uninhabited island, Lars instructed Jilly on the use of the Danforth anchor. "It's an American design. It stows easily. We must make sure you know how to use it."

HELGA CAME LESS frequently, and Lars and Jilly's lunches suffered. He brought a can of beer and a bratwurst for each of them. Jilly looked up after finishing the spare offerings. "Lars, do you want to fuck me? Has Jacobsson ordered you not to, or has he said you could but you don't want to." Lars blushed under his tan. He climbed awkwardly aboard the boat dragging the anchor after him. The sail back to the dock went without incident, and Lars gave few commands. Jilly helped him tie up for the night.

Next morning, Jilly rolled over toward Lars. He had grown gray stubble overnight. "Lars, I have only one request. Clean clothes and underwear every day. No t-shirts. If you don't have enough changes, I will buy them for you. Take off those flip flops before you come to bed. Better still throw them away. They smell awful. And tell Willy to have the sheets changed every three days."

"Of course, Jilly, anything you ask." He opened the door to the hallway. "Willy has rolls and coffee."

Lars instructions grew a shade gentler even than they had been. Jilly manned the tiller on the northern leg. "We are running before the wind Jillian. Tiller a little to starboard and open the mains'l a bit." She accomplished both quickly but awkwardly. "You are safe. Take advantage of the wind, it is strong, but steady" Lars smiled and did not scold. It was a quiet voyage to their picnic island. Neither said much. A few minutes later, a puff of wind came up, and she bore off without Lar's suggestion.

There was a head aboard, but Lars almost forbade its use. It took time and effort to clean, and he was accustomed to more primitive means. Jilly grew to anticipate the landings; she could judge the distance to the spot where they would anchor as the bottom became clearer. She lowered sails by herself, pulled up the Centerboard, and heaved the anchor over the side. "Well done, Jillian. We are here on the sand, and you did not destroy my boat."

After the first few days, Lars had pronounced Jillian a natural, an einsiger (one of a kind), to anyone dockside who cared to listen. He enjoyed watching Jilly's body flex and strain with wind and sail. In return, Jilly taught her rough man of the sea the ways of a lady. He was surprised. Chance, the only thing that mattered, had pushed him toward discovery and different pleasures. Lately he had those aplenty.

CHAPTER 14

Helga

AT ONE POINT, after a week's absence, Helga appeared on the dock at noon as the *Reichenbach* tied up after a calm sail. She smiled like a satisfied parent delighted her children played compatibly in the sand box. "How is the tutoring Lars? I see she hasn't drowned or broken a limb"

"Splendid Helga. We make a good team. Perhaps next summer we can turn the corner and get to the North Sea. It's very different there."

"I must take her away for a while now, Lars. Jillian, I have great news. The tour that I wanted leaves tomorrow morning early. It will last a week, but if we find a place we like, we can break off and stay." Jilly dissected Helga's brief announcement and found an order underneath the sunny tones. She and Lars spent a silent evening. Passion had turned to ease.

In the morning, they rose and drank their thick coffee. They were content when Helga arrived unannounced in her VW. She had already breakfasted. "I am glad you warned me; I have some Americans who want the boat this afternoon." With this lie, he turned his head away.

They went to the boat for her last lesson, and as he stood by the wheel, anger, despair, acceptance, the gratification of survival, and the vapid pleasure of sweaty thighs comprised the spectrum of his emotions. He had felt something new—disappointment in a sea of happiness. By habit, he always picked out natural adversaries upon entering a room. He wanted to know who would pull a knife at the end of a card game. He was almost always right. He had sensed that Jilly danced at the end of Helga's string, and Helga suddenly become a hated rival. She was taking something that he badly wanted. Jillian kissed him on the cheek and climbed from the boat. Lars stared after them and kicked a nonexistent piece of debris.

THE TWO WOMEN got into the car. It smelled of a tobacco. A picnic basket rested in the back seat. Jilly rode silently for miles, again under the microscope. They turned onto the autobahn. "Are we staying only in Germany? No France or Italy?

"No. We have good documents and cover stories for Germany and Denmark. They are very detailed and will hold up under any questioning. We must stay away from courts, which have paper trails, and hospitals, which collect blood types and

DNA. Creating covers for other countries is expensive and time consuming. We all want you on the job a soon as possible.

"We will head down along the Mosel River. And the Rhine. There are vineyards on the Mosel's hillsides that you should know for your cover story of having spent a few years wandering around Europe. Some of the wines are excellent. I will order in German so that we don't get the tourists' pig wash. We will stop where no cameras photograph everything that moves. We should split up when we stop to see a museum or church."

"I would like to visit Rome and Florence. A little detour would not upset our schedule. Bernini is my favorite. There is sculpture there I have seen only in pictures. I want to see Michelangelo's David. The head is marvelous. Haven't you ever been to Rome and Florence, Helga?"

"You know I cannot not tell you anything about my background except that I am native German and speak good, but not perfect, Danish."

There is little more dangerous than innocence, Jilly thought. "The Hermitage doesn't have significant Bernini, and I want to see some sculpture. There's the head of an enraged man or a cursed man in the church of … I don't know which, that perfectly resembles an acquaintance at Yasenevo."

"Jilly." Helga barked "that word no longer exists in your vocabulary. Bury it." Jilly leaned back and inhaled. "Helga, you know so much about me, even things that I don't know. But I am trusting you on someone else's say so. I want to know a few things about you. Where are you from? Are you married? Children? Are you a full-time minder?"

"Jilly, you insult me. The answers to your questions remain my business. I would violate security if I answered. I do this job with very specific instructions from our leaders. I know that your boss values you and your mission. He entrusted a strong mind and body to me to prepare for a difficult assignment. I will not make mistakes. I change my hair, dress, and car after each trip. I never frequent the same places too soon after a previous stay or for very long and never in the same season. I speak Danish only in Northern Germany and change my German accent to accord with wherever I find myself. I change shoes because each change affects my walk. I can hobble along or walk out like a soldier. In conversation, I alter my tastes in music, beer, and art. I never discuss politics. Those are some of the ground elements of tradecraft. We will see if you have learned all your lessons and can put them into effect. I will teach you how to use these tools so that you will survive in a country that is foreign to you and where you must become a new person if you are to complete your mission."

"Helga, you have no weapons, not even concealed needles. Your belt buckle is unusable. I looked. I weigh five kilos less then you, and I am much faster. My training is better and more recent. If you get me into trouble, I will take appropriate measures. It takes nine seconds. You will never know it. I will be in Russia long before your body is found."

"They told me you might say that."

Jilly let the silence grow. Helga, she concluded, was no better than the Armenian smugglers she shot on the beach that night. She finally spoke. "Another sculpture has no resemblance to anyone I know. I have only a poor reproduction of it. It is a three-figure work of a child being nursed by a sheep, and a wild satyr stands by laughing. It is in the Borghese Museum. I wonder why such benevolence is placed beside vengefulness and evil." Jillian wandered back to her father's Sunday lunches.

Helga headed south on the west bank of the Rhine. "Jillian, we will go good, better, best. First, we will visit the smallest town on my list of favorites—the mountain village of Kiedrich, probably fifteenth century. Saturday is the big day there; almost everyone comes in to buy, sell, and drink beer. We had better have some rules. Both of us cannot drink too much on the same day. You have a boyfriend back in Copenhagen. He is a sailor, he is away. You love him and are monogamous. This a religious town. The inhabitants do not know the phrase Marxist dialectic.

"First to the Weingut. He has awful wine for the tourists." Once there, Helga told the mustached old man that she and her companion wanted a carafe of good wine. "Schloss Eltz, if you have it." The old man understood and brought a jug of deep yellow wine from his back room.

"Jillian, we are in the middle of the best Rhine wines in the world. You must know something about wines when you circulate among your fancy friends in America."

"We had only terrible red wine from Georgia at home. When I was young, I would empty the glasses from my father's parties, pour them into one glass, and get sick. I thought that drinking that awful wine was a rite of passage." Helga sipped expertly and passionately. Jillian drank by the mouthful and earned a look of sadness from her friend.

That night the two found a Bierstube that offered massive steins of beer, a band that played drinking songs, and a long bench against the longer wall. If a customer wished to sing and sway next to someone, whoever he or she was, the drinker would simply walk up to the bench, break into the chain of swayers, and join in. Jilly invaded the row of farmers in their best blue suits and sat down with her stein. She smiled, swayed, and drank. Shortly, an American looked down at her. "Mind if I join" He was handsome, well dressed, and spoke American English. He bought a refill for Jillian and himself and picked up the swayers' rhythm after a few gulps of froth. "Why don't we sit at your friend's table?" Jilly smiled her agreement. The American claimed to be an army major who was just finishing a course of treatment at Landstuhl, the military hospital before returning to his regular assignment. Helga drank lightly. They exchanged normal tourists' chatter. "Why don't I buy a bottle of Kummel, and we can go somewhere we can hear each other talk?" Helga nodded in silent approval. The soldier bought the Kummel, took three small badly colored glasses, and they went to

Jilly and Helga's hotel, retrieved their keys, and mounted the stairs. "You two go on. I'm tired. See you in the morning. Nice to meet you, Jimmy" The American said a formal good night to Helga.

"WELL, JILLY?" Helga tried to be nonchalant. "How was your evening, or should I say night?"

"He was a gentleman, Helga. He wore clean clothes, smiled, and showed me the scar from his operation. He is divorced and has two children who live with their mother in Kansas City, Kansas. I don't think he is a spy for the Americans, British, or Germans. He doesn't know much about Europe for having been here two years. I explained that I would probably return to North America one day. I am sure he wanted to see me again, but I dulled that by mentioning my distant Lars, who awaits me in the north."

They packed. Jilly used her credit card to pay the bill. She signed her new and, she hoped, last alias. "You drive, Jilly. It is only a few kilometers to Wiesbaden. Go slowly. Helga gestured. The wine we drank comes from these vineyards. The castle up on that hill is called *Schloss Eltz*. It is a monument to what men can do when they put their minds to it. Very German in that respect. It had probably a dozen architects, and each added his own notion of what a castle on the Rhine should be. It dates from the twelfth century, and the family of one of the original builders occupies part of the building. The wines can be very expensive. Last night, we had a medium-sweet wine called an *auslese*. The grapes were late picked. The sugar content was high."

"Why the interest in grapes and wine, Helga?"

"When I grew up, we had no wine, only beer. I married an encyclopedia of wine. He wasn't much good for anything else. Turn left onto the main road. When we get to the hotel, sign the same way each time, as you signed the credit card. We want to leave a light trail if anybody reads about our little trip. I have many more training trips before I retire, a few will likely be in this neighborhood, and I don't want to stand out during any of them. I have never stayed at this hotel. Repetition often breeds carelessness. It is always good to appear curious about new surroundings."

"Helga, do you mean that you have no home, that you live in hotels, that you don't buy a handsome dress for a concert or go out with friends for a good meal? Who are your friends besides passengers like me?" Only road noise sounded in the car.

"Jilly, you have little understanding of how it was. My family and I lived in the East. The only heat came from the stove and the fire place. We almost starved. I had no little statues or pictures on my bureau, only a little dish of soap. West German prosperity glistened over that wall. We could feel it, see it, but not live it. Now I have a good job and that is the reality, a good job. I worked briefly for the Stasi. When I left I stole most of my records, and a friend excised the rest from the archives. I got clean and a new job. I am not a spy, only a teacher for certain operatives who will be posted in North America and Great Britain. Odd, isn't it, that I have never traveled to

America and only for a short time in England. I liked Scotland. My children are safe in good schools. When I retire, they will visit me with their children. Maybe after your adventures in America, you will too.

"A few little excitements come my way, but I try to keep them at a minimum. Someone else pays for my travels, my Riesling, and my sailing with you and Lars. I love Germany, my children, and the castles along the Rhine. They go together. I like you too, Jilly, and I hope you walk a safe road wherever you land. Clever young people often get into trouble of their own making." Helga's counsel was more fussy than acid. A mother hen clucked through the Sluzhba's teacher of tradecraft's wiles.

The hotel was built on a site that had been leveled by bombs. A speculator had bought the land from the government of Hesse and built a small hotel overlooking the Great Park. Gardens were sacrificed to rentable rooms. The furniture was modern, Spartan, and easy to clean. The doors to the rooms were solid and swung without a squeak. Tourists liked that.

Two small children played quietly in the lobby as Helga and Jilly checked in. A perilous thought came to Jilly. She had never read American children's stories or learned the local games. She would be a fish out of water when her friends of similar age spoke of bringing up their toddlers. She knew that word in English, but the extensive connotations surrounding it had not been part of her curriculum. She remembered from movies that American mothers had an identifiable twist of their bodies when bending over to speak with their children. Was it a learned habit, a social necessity inculcated at a fashionable school, or a way of isolating one's own child from another parents? She made a note that she must learn terms of empathy for the young mothers whom she would meet in America. Even less did she know the folk stories that little Canadians, as she was supposed to have been, had in their blood? Her trip to her notional grandparents' grave would be brief. *But what if some Canadians live near my new home?*

CHAPTER 15

Rothenburg ob der Tauber

HELGA DROVE the entire way from Wiesbaden to Rothenburg. They stopped at one dreary inn after another, though Helga always managed to dredge up a decent Riesling from their cellars. "Safe, I was here two years ago," she said as she examined the wine that accompanied their very ordinary meal.

Amid a week of polite chatter during which Helga ordered Jilly to recite the details of her passport, Helga showed an uncompromising, even frantic, need to arrive at a new, and if one were to believe the expressions on her face, consequential destination. She drove ferociously on twisty back streets where houses touched the curb and on a stretch of autobahn that threatened life and limb. Jilly was almost frightened.

"Here, Jilly is a fairy-tale town. It dates from at least from 804. The streets are marvelous, and except during high tourist season, uncrowded." Helga went on with a passionate disquisition on its social and architectural history. "It is beautiful is it not? Rothenburg was a so-called free town during the middle ages, and because of this, it was coveted. So fortifications were built, and a corps of military men lived here. Walls were built and men assigned to guard various sections of the perimeter in accordance with how effective the individual fortifications were thought to be. The tailors' guild was assigned the back and weaker wall, where the leaders of the day believed the enemy would never come. But the enemy brought ladders tall enough to let its soldiers climb over the barriers. The few surviving citizens made their own clothes for several decades.

"You can nod off to sleep if you want, Jilly, but there are more fascinating stories. The people ran out of water during the sieges, and the surrenders that followed thirst led enemies to rape, burn, and steal. In the thirteenth century, the town laid pipes in secret places so the townspeople could wait out an attack for years if they had enough food. Over time, only the mayor and the water keeper still knew the pipes' locations."

"Who was the man you knew in Rothenburg?"

"What do you mean?"

"The man with whom you fell in love and who made you fall in love with Rothenburg"?

"I did not fall in love with anyone in Rothenburg."

"I will take you at you word. But what is the story? Remember, I am an intelligence officer."

Helga paused, lost her face's color, and surrendered out of female intimacy rather than narrative compulsion. She had also come to believe that preparing Jilly well was more important than adhering to statecraft's rules about what she must not reveal. "It is not so complicated. I had a male passenger for a five-week indoctrination trip. He worked for an American electronics company. He was assigned to go to Russia, Germany, and Switzerland, and we needed to set up his plumbing, his safe houses, addresses, bank accounts, and contacts.

"He was an expensive asset. We wanted never to see him again. He had a regular job, a good one with perks, a wife, and three children. He lived near New York City and had more money than he needed, but he wanted for some reason to become a spy. His ideological mindset belonged to us. He was a strange fellow in that respect, a prosperous businessman who yearned to work for the other side. He never entered a Sluzhba building and met only a few of us under aliases in cities that were his natural business stops. It was a very unusual self-recruitment."

"What happened?"

"You should know the story. We will never meet again nor will you meet any of the people involved. It was sad. He fell in love with me. He wanted to leave his wife and family, move to Europe, and work for us full time. We had enough blackmail material on him to keep him under control. But his wife discovered he was interested in someone else and had gotten involved in some sort of espionage, though not for whom.

"My boss and I decided that he was a potential threat to us and to the secrecy of his mission. We ate late one night, and the restaurant parking lot was dark. I had parked near the back. I opened the boot and pretended to look for a scarf. He bent over to help me, and I gave him potassium chloride. He fell into the trunk, and I lifted his legs inside. I drove to a little-used bridge and dumped him into the Rhine. I took the money from his wallet to make it look like a robbery and wiped his wallet. There was nowhere else I might have left fingerprints. His body traveled far downstream before it was discovered two days later. The police investigated, but nothing important turned up. He had used his credit card for the meal, but the waitress couldn't describe me. I went inactive for a few months, played with my children, drank some good wine, and slept.

"Forget this story, Jillian. The whole affair is distasteful to me. I disliked killing him, but he threatened my existence, my children's way of life, the mission, and my career. He got in way over his head with his two jobs and with me. It was inevitable that the game would end as it did. By the way, Jillian, I am growing fond of you and believe you to be a true and loyal servant of the Sluzhba."

Jillian turned to look at her. "Thank you, Helga.

"What do you say to your children when you return from a mission that involved a death? You can't kill a person without feeling something inside you that shows on the outside. Tell them, 'I've killed a man. I'm tired, now go watch the TV?'"

"No, Jilly, they go to good schools. There is order in their lives. They have my genes. They know that I travel and that the money I make goes mostly for their school, their trips, their food, their house, their clothes, and all the things that matter to them. Each time I leave, I give them strict instructions about their rooms and their studies. When I return, I visit their teachers for updates. They do well. I know their friends' parents. I take a few months off every year to be with them. We hike together.

"We live in a cocoon, and when I return from a trip I must not re-enter the cocoon as an intruder. That will be a difficult trick when they become full-blown teenagers. I think the good will we are building now will survive. They know that I want them to attend university, get married, and have children. They know that I want a comfortable old age with my grandchildren around me."

"Helga, what happens if you don't survive one of your trips?"

"The service and Frau Neuhaus will care for them. That has been arranged."

"How do you account for your income and fancy schools?"

"Everyone knows that I had a husband with a minor title and a rundown castle on the Rhine. Around here that is important. They think he left me enough to get on if I got a small job. Look quickly! Do you see the small river we just crossed? Our meal comes from there tonight."

They checked into the Hotel Eisenhut. Jillian slept in the best bed she ever had. The sheets were inexplicably soft and the blankets light as air. The ceiling had little rococo decorations that looked like birds about to fly away. The mirror above her dressing table was rimmed in gold paint. She toured the designs on the red and green rug that massaged her bare feet. She tried and failed to explain to herself the perversity of the often heartless Sluzhba training that had led her to this luxurious room. Why am I here?

The knock on the door was firm and insistent. Helga stood there in an elegant black dress. Jillian's German vocabulary for haute couture failed her. She could not find a compliment even in Russian. "Don't be surprised, Jilly. I always carry a simple black dress to wear when the occasion arises." She twirled before Jilly and glowed. Jilly realized the snake was dead, but its tail still wriggled. Jillian wore a good but hardly fashionable rich tourist's sweater and long skirt.

They were seated near a window. The sun shone through a voluptuous but orderly garden. No one in Saint Petersburg had the time, money, or space for anything like it. The head waiter moved the vase of flowers and brushed his hand near Helga's shoulder. He handed a menu to Helga and then, with a short glance, to Jilly. Helga caught the attention of several middle-aged gentlemen and returned the gaze of fewer. *What's going on here? I'm better looking than Helga. And younger.* Jillian slipped an American accent into her good German, but to no avail. No one responded with gesture or glance. *This must be German night.*

"Tonight we will eat trout from the little river I pointed out. These are the most delicious in Germany. And we will have *Franken Wein*. It comes only from this tiny area and," the wine waiter brought up a bottle almost on cue, "is bottled in a Boxbeutel, a four-sided wine bottle, the only one of its kind in existence. By German law no other region is allowed to manufacture and use this shape." Neighbors were less interested in Boxbeutels than in Helga's hair, white shoulders, and décolletage. Glances furtive at first, then open, came from every man, and some of the women, in the room. She had triumphed in the elegant kingdom of this dining room, and the wives there stared at their plates. The meal ended with tiny glasses of Kummel. Helga retained her upright posture and lectured Jilly on the wines of the Moselle and the Rhein.

They avoided the elevators and walked up the splendid staircase to their rooms. Outside Jilly's door, Helga turned, took Jilly's shoulders, pressed into her body, and kissed her full on the mouth. Jilly clung to Helga's white shoulders and responded in kind. "It was a very good evening, Jilly."

"Yes, it was." They opened the doors to their bedrooms. At Yasenevo and in English House, Jilly had gotten to know others, their preferences, and habits. Now she traveled alone with a woman whose main trait was anonymity varnished with a profound knowledge of the Riesling grape.

QUIET REIGNED on the trip back to Copenhagen. Jilly drove through towns and villages that Helga selected, most on the map, a few not. Jilly learned to slow down at country crossroads and drive furiously on the autobahn. She surprised herself with a sadness that their journey and companionship were ending. They ventured off the direct route to the coast and dined at Helga's choices. Although the meals and the wines were good, they had lost their zest.

Their conversation almost ceased. Helga's hair lost its perfection, and Jilly wore the same bland outfit for several days. Neither spoke of the other's fall from grace. They both knew that an indefinable and mysterious sliver of their lives had passed. Helga knew what boat would take Jilly back to Copenhagen, from which port, and when.

Jilly knew the date approached. Helga almost stopped speaking. Her directions were rare and muted. She helped Jilly unpack at the boat's gangplank. "We will probably never see each other again, Jilly. This month has been a great pleasure for me." She kissed Jilly on both cheeks and turned away. Jilly, silent, stopped and watched as the car that had been her first home in a foreign land lumbered past the cranes and parked trucks to God knows where.

CHAPTER 16

Return

JILLY RETURNED to St. Petersburg from Hamburg on a boat filled with students on low-cost package tours. She tried to look sullen and distracted. She walked two blocks from the dock. A dusty green car picked her up and drove her to a small airport. She flew on a twin-engine plane to Moscow, and a car drove her to the gate of English House. A guard in civilian clothes turned on the lights, opened the gate, and limped toward her. His arm and shoulder were locked. *Another Afghani*, she mused. *I have returned.* She put her passports, credit cards, and driver's license into a large envelope, passed it to the silent man, and went to the chief's office.

Though night, he was waiting for her. "A good trip, Jilly?"

"I think so, Chief."

"You did not bring back any diseases with you? Good. Any wounds or medical problems?" He waited. "Sleep, and we will talk in the morning. Your room is different from your last. It is in the little white house along the back fence, out of the way. From now you will live in isolation here. Your breakfast and supper will be brought to you. We prefer that you not talk to anyone except us." He opened the door, and a young close-shaven man led her to her quarters. She slept uneasily.

In the morning, her breakfast waited outside her door. At English House, she had always made her own coffee and eggs in early light after she had run five kilometers and before others cluttered up the kitchen. The coffee left for her tasted like brown water, and the rolls were left over from somebody's supper. She changed into American underwear, dress, and shoes and returned to the chief's office.

He leaned forward and folded both hands on his desk. After a silence meant to establish his control, he instructed: "For the next few weeks you will work in the language lab. The American major you met is a PhD linguist from Pittsburg. He reported that your English is almost perfect. But your c's are often misplaced. Remember that the c in citadel, cut, and church are pronounced differently."

Jilly erupted: "That bastard! He drank half a bottle of my Kummel."

"Little mistakes get you maimed or killed Jilly. After some work in the language lab at hours when no one else will be there, you will return to Willy's in Copenhagen, where you will not find Lars and the *Reichenbach*, because he will have taken a group of Americans to the sailing races in Malmo. You will complain that the conniving bastard promised you a trip to those same races but reneged for American money. You will drink a little and let everyone know you think it is time to return to America. Then you will fly to Montreal by way of New York, thence to Winnipeg to visit your grandparents' graves, and finally, via Boston, to Nantucket Island, where you will deposit two-hundred-thousand dollars from Deutsche Bank into the account you will open at the Bank of Sconset. You will look for a house and buy it. A new life in a very comfortable part of the world. Not everybody gets that chance."

Jilly rose. "Chief, have you ever heard the name Krushkin?"

"Never, Jillian. Now get on with it." Jilly spent ten days in the language lab. An instructor heard every word through her ear phones and critiqued Jilly regularly.

THE CHIEF WORE a dark blue suit as a symbol of authority. Or because the day was unseasonably chilly. Mary Ellen guessed he felt cold wherever he stood. He posed behind the stern oak desk and shifted papers as though clearing his mind for a major proclamation. "What I am about to discuss with you embodies many elements of state policy. Over that, we exercise little control. We, you and I, are tools of the state. Poison, death, killings, assassinations are all part of our craft—just as wrenches and torches fill a plumber's bag. We have trained you to collect the contents of Professor Ingraham's brain, and to accomplish that, you must enter his milieu while you go about your work. How I envy you Nantucket, Cape Cod, and Provincetown.

"Here I must become a lawyer. The state believes in and practices what we call targeted killings. These occur after the most thoughtful deliberations. The benefits and the risks, the long-term and short-term effects on us, our allies, and our enemies are finely calculated.

"Jillian, we want to eliminate those who call the shots for the opposition. To do so, we want the professor's addition to the nasty weapons of conflict. The quiet men start wars. They convince their people that military engagements that will likely end in mass slaughter are viable methods. We want to relieve them of their capacity to perpetrate harm. We want them to know that they live in mortal or at least incapacitating danger if they continue their bellicose ways. Ingraham doesn't give a fig about international politics or Russia's survival. We do.

"The decision to take such action must have two components: very sophisticated technology, that is your job, and a well-reasoned argument for setting the plan in motion. That job belongs to the *Vashni*. Some states are unable to live at peace with their neighbors or with anyone else."

"I know chief. It's the same in the barracks."

"To yield to them is to surrender to their savagery. Savages will make mistakes— they want too much too soon, and they fail to understand the ultimate consequences of their actions. Our former enemies were logical; our present enemies lack that property. You have become the instrument for balancing others' evil with the interests of Russia, your state." He slumped. "Russia has lived for centuries by war and revolution. I wonder if it enemies will ever behave differently."

"SOON YOU will leave the shelter of English House. I hope it has been a pleasant stay. For us, we have enjoyed having you as our guest."

He loves this place, Jilly thought. *He's a minor Russian nobleman of the nineteenth century, retired to his family farm. He visits Tsar Krushkin once a year to show his face and get his orders. The old Russia with a new mask! He wants to stay until his retirement and even then, Krushkin will have to evict him.*

"Soon you must win the affection and confidence of a different race who speak a different language with different nuances of thought and psychological reactions. For example, an American says my child was killed yesterday in a car accident. That is a horrible event in anyone's life. The American will weep and expect tears in your eyes. We here, especially those of my and your father's generation, would say: 'Yes, awful!' but would also be thinking, *Of course, I lost my entire family in a village near Kursk. I saw an artillery shell decapitate my best friend near Berlin just as the war ended. My first child died because no blood was available in that hospital.* Did you know that Brezhnev couldn't get antibiotics for his wife from the Kremlin's pharmacy even though you and I could buy them on the street?

"Once you land in America you must get on and remain on a new wavelength. We played games here in English House that were as realistic as we could make them. We have trained you and tested you to expect the unexpected. So there is no bad luck, only the unexpected, and such occurrences will usually originate from your colleagues.

"Our lessons were your basic training. You are about to enter what the Americans call the Real World. An astute person will notice any awkward social reactions the first time and, by the third error on your part, conclude that you are not who you pretend to be. We are not scientists who scoff at four or five failed experiments because we know the fifth will lead to success. Prudence is not an option or a sign of subservience or humility or weakness. It is a necessity until your feet rest firmly on the ground. And then afterwards, as well. When your neighbors and acquaintances accept you for what you pretend to be, with all your eccentricities, you can proceed on your mission."

"What is my mission, Chief? After all this training, what am I supposed to do? I know I won't be translating newspaper articles in the basement of the Dzershinsk Square I know the unexpected will happen, but what am I expected to accomplish?"

"Our mutual friend Krushkin barely tipped the surface of your job in America. Last time I saw him he wasn't wearing a colored shirt. A button-down collar, I recall. Neither was he wearing glasses."

"Without a colored shirt, tie, and glasses he must look like a Mongol warrior. He is very darkly complected."

"I didn't say he wasn't wearing a colored tie, Jillian. You must notice these details in others' speech."

"Of course, Chief."

"Since his remarks to you, more has happened. Your mission, as we have explained to you, is to harvest whatever advances Professor Ingraham has made in the field of germs and all information he has about how to exploit them— when, where, how, and with what intensity and scope. He leaned back and stretched his arms. This was the first time Jillian had seen him break his elegant posture. Or perhaps he wanted to show his gold cuff links.

"Professor Ingraham has climbed to the top of the germ world. The metaphor is bad, I know. He will probably not win a Nobel, but not for lack of his sycophantic efforts. I'm afraid that even his wife's money can't buy that. We are up to date on his researches, thanks to a combination of our hackers' skills and Ingraham's desire to let the world know of his cleverness. He can probably produce a germ bomb. We know that. What we don't know is how far he has gotten in developing a communications link and a remotely detonated fuse. Our electronics section can build a basic fuse. Connecting the fuse to the packets of different sizes, content, and purpose is as yet unknown to us. It is not a matter of pillow talk, regrettably. His fuse, if he has it, will be a matter of formulas, mathematical symbols, and matters of which I am entirely ignorant. Perhaps you will recognize or decipher some of the research.

"Your specific task is to enter his computer or computers, copy the materiel onto a thumb drive that will be sent to you in Boston, and return that full thumb drive to us. It is a special memory stick that leaves no clue that you have invaded his computer. How you accomplish that task, I can only imagine. You must arrange, on your own initiative, many visits to his office in order to harvest the data as he proceeds with his work. Or, if he has already designed the device, it might be that only one pass at his data will reward you with that dacha near your father's in Sochi."

"Why a remote detonator, Chief?'

"Let us propose that we have under surveillance twenty-five persons of interest who can do incalculable harm to Russia. We want to put in place germs, toxins, or whatever we might use to exterminate them or cause a sickeningly large penalty should they continue their nefarious ways. We would kill or harm many fewer innocent people than we would by using those hundreds of missiles that we both have. The gold mines of South Africa, the oil fields of the North Sea, or a simple odious tribal leader in his thatched hut are targets that come readily to mind. After we have placed the germ bomb, for lack of a better description, we want to be able to detonate it from a satellite, from a submarine, from the Kremlin's bathroom, or from anywhere on earth or in space. Getting the information we need to accomplish that very tricky but necessary task is your job. That is all I have to say, Jillian Augusta Carlson."

A CLERK ESCORTED her to her room, sat down on the bed, and read a check list aloud.

"Passports, cavity for Copenhagen dentist, Danish and German cosmetics, German underwear." He droned on for an hour. Potassium chloride lipstick, ricin knitting needles, and the rest of her emergency kit would be sent to her later via her Boston contact once she was safe in place. She flew to St. Petersburg, boarded a trawler, and after a few tranquil hours at sea, transferred to a sailing boat and landed at a sleepy harbor in Eastern Denmark. She drove to Willy's and got her old room.

She walked the docks she had walked with Lars and complained to the hands of other boats that he had left with tourists. She asked Willy to make a one-way reservation to Montreal, from where she would travel west to see her grandparents' graves.

THE PLANE ROLLED down the runway, clonked the wheels into the hull, and took off for Canada. Jilly had left her belongings and favorite volume of Pushkin, all tagged, in the locker for departing students and read a paperback from the airport shop. She bought The New York Times and The Washington Post. She had learned much of American politics and read the papers easily. A few children cried themselves to sleep. The gay steward took a fancy to a handsome, tanned American and asked him every thirty minutes if he wanted water, a newspaper, or anything else. The passenger finally allowed that he was not interested, and the steward walked sadly to his other targets and responsibilities.

Jilly found the air disturbing. She knew the feel and smell of the wind in Moscow, Copenhagen, Petersburg, and in the Baltic. She could tell where she was. The air beside the stream and battlements of Rothenburg had established their own presence and aroma. The air inside the plane felt unhealthy and unfit for city dweller and peasant alike. It was void of any possibilities beyond its use on that airplane. She longed for the smell of Russian earth after a rain. Any earth after a rain. After passing through customs and immigration, Jilly waited fitfully for the ride to Winnipeg. She hadn't slept decently for a day and a night.

THE CEMETERY attendant gangled across the wooden floor to investigate his first inquirer of the day. Jilly showed him a newspaper clipping and said, "Could you help me? My grandparents are buried here, but I don't think I can find my way to their gravesite."

"Carlson, there are so many Carlsons here." The young man smiled and dragged a thick deed book from a shelf. "When were the deceased interred?"

"About fifteen years ago."

"Ah, here it is. Lot 120." He drew a circle on a map of the cemetery and handed it to her. Jilly thanked him without a smile and walked to the graves. The Yasenevo crowd told me to expect the unexpected, but checking in with people she had never known struck her as eerie. *One of the poets must have written about it,* she thought and recalled from the recesses of her forbidden Russian mind that one of Pushkin's gypsies said: "I am brave, I fear neither knife nor fire." She took a flower from another grave and placed it over the never-known couples' remains.

CHAPTER 17

Boston

SHE FLEW BACK to Montreal's Dorval airport and headed to Boston. The flight was bumpy. The sky was beautiful and blue. Her luggage got lost. She waited two hours at Logan for the bags to come in on the next flight from Dorval. They looked more battered than when she had delivered them to the security bin in Copenhagen, and they smelled different. Jilly used a pay phone from the concourse to call Jerry Mayfield, the Sluzhba's support officer in Boston. He used Yasenevo's coded language to tell Jilly to register at an expensive motel and come to his office on Dartmouth Street at eleven the next morning after checking out of her room.

Mayfield had placed put ads in the personals columns of half-a-dozen computer magazines describing a job seeker proficient in a range of critical software packages and with detailed knowledge of European and American/British accounting and business practices. The clerks, who knew him from previous calls, assumed he was trying to place another degree candidate who had spent the year's tuition money on pot and good restaurants. Jerry Mayfield matched calls for services with graduate students, retirees, and housewives looking for work. This cover proved to be a boon when Jilly came on the scene. He would be able to find her work himself. He was well known in the computer community around Boston and Cambridge and took fifteen percent from those he rented out and five from the companies he had them serve. He worked from a shabby office on Dartmouth Street and rarely met the people or businesses he matched.

Treachery can hide in signals between operatives who have not met. Jillian had memorized each word and all the punctuation marks of this first exchange before she left English House, and she compelled Mayfield to repeat his instructions to the last comma. She avoided a filled elevator and climbed the stairs to his office. It was clear that he never intended to interview proper citizens in this ill-kept suite of two rooms and two desks, one for himself and one for the secretary he never hired. The dye of his red leather sofa had worn off in spots to show dirty white underneath. Publicity pictures of former governors of Massachusetts hung in disconsolate frames. Two diplomas from a defunct college in Montana swung opposite the couch. Childrens' drawings dotted the walls.

When she knocked, a tall thin man in well-worn shoes and a blue wash-and-wear shirt appeared unsteadily in the doorway. His collar was open and he had dirty finger nails. He looked surprised to see an attractive young woman who appeared far more composed and striking than the few of his clients he sometimes met. Jillian took out a pad and wrote, "Swept? Turn off cell phone and computers. Remove SIM card from cell phone. Speak only English."

Mayfield nodded. "Pleased you saw my ad. Glad to have a new worker bee. Things have been quiet here lately." Jillian knew that understatement was the truth. His position was a non-job for the Sluzhba's logistics and communications department. He had been in place for twenty years and did almost nothing competently. But he knew his turf, and it would be impractical to withdraw him even if he were a model case of burnout.

He turned on a raucous Boston Celtics game. Jilly retreated for a second into her past and remembered the one similar broadcast she had heard at English House. The noise and fleeting images on the television jarred her. But she came back to the present quickly and listened to his routine instructions.

"Your emergency packages will arrive later. All the weapons, disguises, meds and radio. Contact Brackett and Brackett, the real estate firm, and say you saw their ad in Yankee Magazine. Understood? Take a week to find a house. That's about the norm for new arrivals. Your story is that you saw pictures of the island when you were in Europe and found it appealing because you want to be near Boston, but not in it.

"Listen carefully to our contact arrangements. You heard them over there, but I want to make sure." Jilly memorized the normal and emergency contacts. He outlined her emergency exfiltration plan and made her repeat it. "Jillian, please do not cause or become involved in an accident.

"If you get hurt, make an emergency communication. We have a secure doctor. We can bandage wounds and perform minor surgery." Jillian knew most of his tedious instructions from her briefings in Europe. "You know your target and your mission. I cannot add to what you have been ordered." He spoke as though he had been privy to the formulation of the mission and the selection of the person who would complete it. Almost certainly he had been kept ignorant of Jilly's selection for the job and her relationships with Krushkin and the chief. And of the job itself. Her mind stopped following Mayfield's unsympathetic drone.

However entombed by his sloth, Mayfield had accumulated the basic truths of his operational patch and, therefore, of Jilly's. He told her the ways she could get to Nantucket: plane from Boston to the island or plane or bus to Hyannis with plane or ferry to Nantucket. He suggested she familiarize herself with all of them. However precise her briefings in Europe had been, the northeast United States remained new and strange—not foreboding, but mysterious. Helga and Rothenburg and the chief were long gone. Lars remained.

Her instructors at Yasenevo had explained the dangers of her job. None had defined the risks. These would come from people and situations that were foreign to her. A mall where she was new. Credit cards about to expire at the same time. A second generation Slav who recognized the cadences of her syllables. If she were followed should she shake the trailer and so announce her professionalism or let him follow her to home or job? *Am I heading toward the success that the chief wished for me, or is this meeting the first step toward entropy and disaster?*

JILLY DECIDED to take the bus to Hyannis and the ferry to Nantucket. Her elderly seat mate said little and breathed heavily. But the smell of the sea, even though it was contaminated by diesel fumes, lifted her spirits. She scanned her fellow passengers. Dwellers in the gilded simulacra of power declined to admit, although some knew, that sordid events in dingy rooms and flea-filled huts sustained their positions.

One good agent in the right place at the right time could tip the world one way or the other. Hanssen and Philby knew that. The job had its perks. The chief and Krushkin had steeled themselves against others' foppery while displaying their own to all. It was an allowed decoration. In living what universal laws judged to be false, even felonious, lives, they lived truer lives than almost anybody else on earth. They were not superior to others but outside their universe. They did not think like others who failed to understand an opaque universe beyond the ken of all but a few. They knew that they dirtied their hands so that the man with the birth mark on his face could stand immaculate and look his opposites in their own deceitful eyes. It was lonely at times, a fearful life in the middle of an unknowing crowd. That would have been difficult to explain to the passengers of the Hyannis to Nantucket ferry.

CHAPTER 18

A Garden

JILLY DEBARKED and walked past shops beginning to show life after the island's depopulated winter. The innocence of the place struck her as perverse. Perhaps the sea winds kept it lean and fresh. As much as the houses were feathered by great gobs of naked wealth, a certain simplicity survived. She remembered the religious differences of centuries ago, when the Indians belonged to the Congregational Church but refused to pay a minister, and the English fishermen adhered to Quakerism but refused to pay an elder. Perhaps some of that kind of thought survived.

Jilly enjoyed the uphill walk. She had not taken her ten-kilometer run for some time. As much as anything else, that aberration from her routine prompted her purchase of a house in which she could be alone, work alone, and exercise her body as well as her profession.

SHE CAME to a door painted in with so many thick coats of green that the paint presented itself as the door. A dozen layers of color and marine varnish did not need the wood to block the winds and the rain. The paint had begun to chip and show more paint underneath. Two or three years would pass before someone would, probably with reluctance, anoint the wood anew. Jilly went in, and an open-faced man said, "Good morning. I'm Joe Kosciusko. What can I do for you?" They looked at maps of residential areas, both streets where the houses were priced for Wall Street partners and shacks that needed "loving care." Kosciusko was pleasant, and Jillian reciprocated his easy ways.

He recommended a motel, and they scheduled their next day's inspections. She slept that night, but not before conjuring that their ancestors were born probably with a few hundred miles of each other to die in war. The earth did not rest quietly on their graves.

Jilly rose the next morning with the smell of salt in her nostrils, and after breakfast, toured houses. Neither she nor her father had ever been forced to inspect properties in order to decide which among them was the most suitable. City authorities gave them so-many square meters, and that was that. English House had not taught her the joy that accompanies the purchase of an attractive dwelling with someone else's money. Joe showed her palaces, houses, shacks, and raw land.

Jilly flew to Boston with a folder of pictures of houses to consider. She picked a small house she had seen briefly. Set on a back road a few miles from the town's Center, it was isolated from all but a few neighbors, and the dirt road gave adequate warning of anyone's arrival. It had a cellar, a garage, and a walkway where Jilly intended to keep her bicycle in good weather. There was enough land for her to grow her own vegetables, and she thought of duplicating her father's plot at Sochi. The challenge of learning about the soil, suitable plants, and even new kinds of fertilizer and equipment excited her.

The sale gratified Joe Kosciusko, who arranged for Brackett and Brackett's attorney, Charlie Banks, to execute the transfer of title. Jed Gorham dropped in to the Banks office to meet Jillian and congratulate her on her astute purchase. Joe asked if she had any furniture and kitchen gear that he could have shipped over for her.

"No, I'm starting from scratch. I left most of my stuff in Canada before I went to Europe, but I would rather get furniture that fits Nantucket."

"I know just the place," Kosciusko and Banks chimed in simultaneously. Joe continued, "There are people here and in Hyannis who can get you started, and you can go from there. Also, someone always sells out at the end of summer."

"I'll also need garden tools. I could never put roots down while I was traveling. No pun intended." Her father had told her one evening during a dark Petersburg winter that none of his friends had ever lied to one another. He was certain. Now she reminded herself that lying was all she had. Not English, but duplicity had become her new language.

CHAPTER 19

Settling In

JILLY POSTED ADS for her computer and business services in the Nantucket and Hyannis papers. Joe Kosciusko steered an old lady with tax troubles to her, and a family who ran an ice cream shop came to her door. Jerry Mayfield got her an account in Cambridge.

As she built her business, "the new girl" made the rounds of the shops and gathering places of Nantucket. She spent small sums. People saw her as neither rich nor overbearing, just a nice person of moderate means who had settled on the island year round while earning enough to pay the mortgage and buy food. She bicycled everywhere, no car yet, and her red laptop bag was always visible in the side basket or on her shoulder. Against her best instincts, she ate an ice cream cone once a week and wished she had only one job life—the island would be so pleasant. As at Yasenevo, she had longed to be known and favored and feared.

JILLY VISITED MAYFIELD, with whom face-to-face meetings remained necessary. She ordered him to ensure that no other active Sluzhba officer worked on a target in her vicinity. He nodded. "Is that absolute clear Jerry?"

"Yes," he replied in a voice as firm as hers. "Jilly," he intoned as if here were giving a lecture from a public platform, "we have put together a likely schedule for your target, Phillip James Ingraham. How you use it is your affair. If we receive more information on this unlikeable fellow, we will send it to you." Jilly was irritated and let him know it. He was telling her nothing she did not know about tradecraft or Ingraham.

"That is precisely your job, Jerry. You are not my boss. He resides in a gray building far away. You know that. You are to acquire whatever tangible materials I need for my assignment and pass the takes I gather to the cutout. Your secondary task is to keep other members of the directorate away from my patch while I am working. Please don't lecture me on secret writing done with the pee of a dead goat. We are beyond that."

Mayfield continued without missing a beat, reminding her that Ingraham seldom visited his wife, who lived out in the country and had money and financial independence. That he had tenure at Harvard and had no trouble getting grants that stood him in good stead everywhere in his world. Mayfield suggested she walk by

Ingraham's apartment on Pinckney Street. "The professor and his wife rarely socialize together. She likes horse shows and those who frequent them. He likes his work, good restaurants, the admirable museums of Boston, and women who are twenty-five years younger than he. He visits the Museum of Fine Arts or the Gardner at least twice a week, usually around noon, for an hour or two. He prefers the classics: Rembrandt, Vermeer, and such. You know much more about them than I. You will meet him at one of these two places and begin to complete your assignment."

Jilly leaned forward. "Jerry, there is a sign on the library wall of English House: *What is essential is not visible to the naked eye.* I will remain invisible, and I hope you do, too." And dropping into Russian, she muttered "Fuck your mother; stay out of my assignment. I will meet him where I choose to meet him."

Mayfield showed Jilly a recent picture of Ingraham climbing the steps to the second floor of the Gardner. Tall, slightly stooped, handsome, good clothes. A few evenings spent gazing at the Pinckney Street ceiling might well turn out to be more enjoyable than the solitary delights of Nantucket Island.

AND YET ISLAND weekends offered their own delights. She could feel safe, except when she spied Bob Horan, whom she knew to be the local FBI agent, across a room. She felt almost collegial toward him. After all, they both worked for their governments in the same profession—except that he was nominally the hunter and she the prey. He always treated her civilly, nothing more, nothing less. But she was more comfortable when he was not around.

She came to know the social circles of Nantucket—who joined whom for dinners in, dinners out, Saturday afternoon drinks, and token drinks at the tennis club. Gatherings for Jed Gorham's banking friends sat on top of the social hierarchy. Each group guarded its exclusiveness as the walls did Rothenberg. Only very occasionally was a parapet breached.

The wives, which, Jilly observed, was the only way most defined themselves, generally accepted her. A rare awkwardness, fueled perhaps by envy, followed drinks at the tennis club on afternoon. Betty Cawthorn (wife of Bertram) stalked her one evening and, by way of asking after her well-being, offered the proposition that Jilly, a newcomer, must find everything so strange. Jilly was unfazed, and said to her, "Conservatives and liberals, tall and short, just as everywhere. You come from a Tory line don't you? If I recall, your family sent its boats to Boston to help British preparations for the attack on Bunker Hill."

"I don't know about that, but I do know they were whalers."

"And very brave they were. I remember they lost everything in the Great Fire of 1846, rebuilt their fortune, and here you are." Betty Cawthorn turned aside and went for another drink.

It was perfect running weather, and after a good 10K that Sunday, Jilly bicycled around the island's paths and roads. People had begun to recognize her, several waved. She had picked up her emergency cache from Mayfield but had kept it in her house too long for her cautious mind. She could not bury the package close to houses, where it could be detected, or a few miles away, where it would be useless when most needed. It had to be buried deep enough not to emerge in a rainstorm, and the dirt surface had to be put back so that a casual walker would not think to investigate. Most of all, she had to be able to find it if she were pursued or wounded or both.

When she was sent to practice the task in Kiev, she had found a derelict wall in a slum. The wall had a hole that she could cover with brick. She put her kit into the wall, surrounded it with every bit of metal she could gather, and bricked it in. Assuming she was being observed, she tied up her leg so that she limped to the railroad station for her foodless trip to Moscow. The cache had a GPS in it so the instructors could locate it. It took hours of reading distorted signals to find the package. A few instructors were furious. More than a few were delighted at the progress shown by their star pupil.

On her Sunday evening ride along Nantucket's Milestone Road, Jilly turned into a small thicket of pine trees. Nobody had been on the cycling path or the roadway. She took off her vest and rolled it into a ball to be a marker. She moved the bicycle twenty meters into the thicket and aligned it at ninety degrees to the path and memorized the tree it rested against and how it rested there. She used her compass to take ninety-degree bearings on two visible structures and prayed that they would stand during her stay on the island. She took her folding shovel from the side basket on her bicycle and dug a hole one-meter deep. No sense in digging farther; the ground was sandy, but dry. If she needed access to the container, she wouldn't have time to mine deeper. The hole was far from the eroding beaches.

The cache contained a .22 caliber pistol, a box of cartridges, and two knives, one with a three-inch blade and one five-inches long. She carefully packed a tiny one-way transmitter whose mishandling would tell the Center that she had been taken or was dead. The medical packet contained a roll of bandage that could hold a one-hundred-kilo human with a need to climb or descend a wall. It resembled duct tape. There was a bottle of tiny pills to keep Jilly awake and alert for seventy-two hours, three ampules of potassium chloride, and three syringes to put a target to sleep forever. Five-thousand dollars and two-thousand Euros were wrapped around three new passports. She placed the package on a stone that she had inserted into the hole, replaced the dirt, and brought the top layer back to the way it had looked. She took her bearings and measurements again and walked back to the path. She put on her vest, waited until no car or cyclists appeared, moved into open view, and pedaled home. The rules demanded she give Mayfield an accurate description of the cache's location. On the next trip, she would be sure to give him a location on the island's other side.

SHE KEPT her training knife all through her travels. It was German made and had perfect balance. Her hands were much stronger than the average computer expert's. Her kind instructor, one of the few at Yasenevo, had taken her on as a private pupil. He told her before she departed that she had reached an exceptionally high level of competence with non-kinetic hand weapons. She could, he wrote, take out two opponents with stick, stone, bottle, or knife. The third would probably get her unless she ran. "Remember the three-foot rule," he always told her. Even if you are on your back and bleeding, there is almost always an item that can be used as a weapon.

CHAPTER 20

Biding Time

A MAN FROM CHICAGO opened an account with a million dollars at the Sconset Bank. Jed thought him brusque, if likeable, but focused more on the simple fact that the man wanted to buy a boat. He had little idea what kind. Jed telephoned a yacht broker, and five days later, the broker returned the call to say he had sold the man a sailboat for almost a million and had lined up a captain and two college students to teach the enthusiastic buyer about rocks and shoals. Jed was delighted—the hefty sum would stay in the bank, merely shifting to the broker's account. Jed had built good will with two depositors as, he complimented himself, a good neighborhood banker should do.

Jed hosted dinner parties from time to time, more to gather useful gossip from his friends than to entertain. Charlie Banks, the Bracketts, and one of the yacht brokers were typically included among the guests. Jilly was flattered to have become a regular. Jed's wife decided one evening to seat James Baxter, a summer visitor, she said, and a university computer expert from upstate New York, next to Jillian. His skin was drawn tightly over high cheekbones. He had combed his full head of hair meticulously. There was an air of severity about him. He stood out from those on the island who toiled for the sake of pleasure.

His deep knowledge rescued him from being labeled boring, but Jilly grew suspicious. He knew a lot about Canada, and Jilly told of her childhood and education there as briefly as she could. *He is getting close to the bone but is too vague about himself. Why no specific employer, no mention of wife and children, and no bragging about degrees or medals or plaques or important academic papers.* Jilly was careful not to look careful. After Gorham closed the door on his departing guests, they shook hands. Jilly cycled to her house, and Baxter returned to his cottage. He did not make a pass or describe his lonely nights away from home.

Jilly thought Baxter an extraordinarily competent programmer and designer of fixes for misbehaving software. She also understood that he had not been talking to her during dinner as much as he was examining her. She had nattered on safely, describing fully and honestly all but one aspect of her work before retreating into respectful silence. The rough ferry trips to Hyannis, the disappointments of starting a new business, and the fun of outfitting a new house drew thin smiles. He answered nothing about children, academic papers, or his favorite baseball team. He was not a domesticated husband.

Back home, Jilly sat at her computer in a woolen robe and searched for Mr. James Baxter of upstate New York. She found a carpenter and three plumbers, several high school teachers, two morticians, and a Baptist minister. She screened Baxter through every test she could dredge from her conscious mind. He failed to show in any. Every peg had its hole in both her businesses, but he fit nowhere. James Baxter lived in the mists somewhere. She wasn't sure she wanted to meet him again.

SHE RECOGNIZED the voice. She had met its owner and his wife at a Nantucket Club party, where he wore a seersucker coat, white-button-down shirt, dark tie, and tennis tan. He had the perfect indefinable American face and manner. He was the American Mr. Everyman pictured in every movie evening at Yasenevo, and that meant he stood out in the throng of both the Nantucket wealthy and the island's eccentrics. His short blond wife had worn a pretty but unremarkable party dress and stood with her shoulders hunched as though preparing to bow before an unseen God.

"Is this Jillian Carlson?" He spoke with an unplaceable accent.

"Yes"

"This is Bob Horan from the island's FBI office. How are you? I believe we met at the club."

"Fine, what can I do for you?"

"I have a situation here that might be right up your alley. Could you come down and talk to me about it?"

"I'm terribly busy. Why don't you come here? If it's not inconvenient."

"All right. I've always wanted to see the office of the island's most celebrated computer person."

"I am not that Mr. Horan, but I will be working here this afternoon. You can come any time before five. I have an engagement at six." That was a lie. She wanted time to test the dishes she planned for a party with the bank crowd. She needed to cook them for herself first. It was good to lie to Horan at the beginning. It put her in the proper mindset for the inquiry about her he was sure to make.

Horan arrived in a dark blue car and climbed the concrete stairs.

"Thanks for your time. What a lovely house! The previous owner didn't take care of it. Very nice place."

"Thank you, Mr. Horan. What can I do for you"?

"It's a strange problem. Some people on the island have noticed unusual stuff going on with their computers. Things like lost files, deleted passwords, and misplaced pages on their Excel programs. Lots of wealth here, and its owners are worried that someone is hacking into their bank and stock accounts. This is a small community, and when folks realized it wasn't only them, they came to me. God knows how long it's been going on. The hypothetical hackers might just be having fun by disrupting families' records, but then again, they might be stealing valuable financial and medical data. I understand you're the local expert. Can you help us figure out what's going on?"

Jilly leaned back in her chair and paused. She knew the bureau had its own cyber theft analysts and that she'd never be called in on a real problem. "None of my clients on the island have had anything like that happen, but then my work here is mostly small businesses not worth hacking. Can I get you coffee?"

"No thanks. Where did you learn all these computer skills? I'm still a blunderer."

"I learned from anyone I could. I took courses in Denmark, of all places, and worked for a small business there. I worked for a hotel in Copenhagen in exchange for a clean room and a big breakfast. The nerds from MIT are much better than I, but they only take on large projects that last a long time. I take the crumbs off the table. Around here, only a few of the crumbs are decent, but they do help pay the mortgage. Still, I need to do more than half my work in Boston."

"Clever lady." He looked at the furniture. "My wife always wanted a Welsh hutch like yours.

"I found it in the backroom of a lawyer I worked for. He was settling an estate and didn't know what he had."

Horan stood. "I smell good cooking. I never know what kind of fish my wife is getting up. By the way, please call me Bob."

She smiled as she opened the door. "Call me Jillian." *At least he didn't ask me where I was born and what I have done with my life. I suppose that comes next.*

THE NEXT DAY, Jilly slung her computer bag over her shoulder and locked her front door. Her neighbor Jonah glanced at her sideways. He kept note of cars passing and domestic noises. He looked at Jilly. "The rye grass has covered the lawn quickly this year. If you want to mow and trim the hedge, I can get someone for you."

He's trying to be polite by pretending he doesn't know I already have someone. Jilly mulled over Jonah Coffin's meddlesome advice for a moment and replied, "You're right. I'll have Manuel cut the grass when I get back. I won't be gone long. I'm bringing back some material I can work on here, and I'll buy a container of weed killer." The renewed awareness that Manuel spent time alone at her house awakened a warning from her training that someone who pawed around her house in her absence was a threat.

JONAH COFFIN was an island character born off-island. Generations of his family had fished and shucked quahogs for as long as anybody in South Chatham knew. He had moved to Nantucket after a stint in the Korean War, bought land at twenty dollars an acre, and fished occasionally, returning to South Chatham for vacations. The old busybody's accent was New England drawl mixed with the clipped syllables of Cape Cod.

He fancied himself the self-appointed dean of the clutch of houses that faced the beach and kept measurements of the sea's annual incursion upon his domain. He lived alone at the end of what had been a forested dirt road that ran through the land he had acquired, a road that officialdom had named against his objections. Jonah's winters were mute, and the winds that scoured the island blew in one side of his shack and out the other. He neither sought nor received invitations, and had he been asked to Jed Gorham's table, he would not have accepted. He had seen a tennis racket once in a store window and hadn't liked what he saw.

Standing on the road outside his shack, Jonah could gauge to a single degree Fahrenheit the progress of warmth in the spring and chill in the fall. Spring set off a feral energy in him that every year ensnared a buyer for a single acre of his land. He chose carefully from the many who sought to own a piece of the island, and he enjoyed reeling in the avaricious buyer more than he had trawling a net full of haddock. With his bank statement burnished by a sum that gladdened him for another year, he bestrode his neighborhood, keeping order among his new neighbors for another turn of the seasons.

He was tall, thin, and strong, and he stood on that line between pain in the neck and valuable neighbor. He had a penetrating voice, and in conversation, he neither embraced his heritage nor expected anyone else to do so. It was good to stay on the right side of Jonah. He liked Jilly for a reason he could not explain to himself, but he also feared her a little.

HE OFFERED suggestions as though they were orders. No one seemed to mind.

"Thanks, Jonah. I know it's a mess now, but I'll get it fixed up." She laughed silently at Jonah's dismissive wave. He often lamented the changes the newcomers had made in fabricating a society and building roads and docks that in the normal evolution of life were never meant to be. Over months, Jilly had wrought simple charms on him. It was not difficult; a clutch of friends did not fill his life. He became favorably impressed and changed his view of her from tidy newcomer to well-mannered lady who might indeed have a prosperous and pleasant future on Nantucket Island.

"Better to cut the weeds before they go to seed. You'll get better grass." She tried to show neighborly interest rather than the irritation she felt at what she considered unwarranted interference in her housekeeping. Jonah Coffin, now a friend, thought of himself as a member of every household on his road.

Even though nothing of importance lay about the house except for an increasing amount of nineteenth-century Philadelphia and Rhode Island furniture, Jilly affected a display of privacy for the neighbors' sake. That is what they expected. Manuel cut the thin rye grass and manicured the few bushes that survived the winters. He often poked around looking, he said, for a nonexistent can of oil that was usually discovered in the back of his pickup. Manuel's son spoke limited English. He trailed behind his father as Manuel cut grass, planted flowers, and filched tools and small bits of hardware.

His father and Jilly considered it an essential part of the unwritten compensation agreement.

Jilly's bright jerseys, shorts, and red sneakers fascinated him, and he came to wonder what lay behind those other worldly coverings that were clean of cod, haddock, and lobster. A cousin had come over from Chatham, and Manuelito had shyly asked his mother: "What is that smell?"

"That is the smell of oysters. Your cousin takes them out of their shells every fall."

Poor lad, Jilly thought. *He doesn't have access to the minds and manners of a dozen or so scientists to educate him on Sundays and train him for the world that will be.*

CHAPTER 21

Backstory

JILLY OPENED the Boston Globe more to keep up with the city's fashions and scandals than to seek news. A city councilman caught in flagrante with his boyfriend, a MacDonald's manager arrested after amassing two-hundred-thirty-five-thousand dollars from his store over six years. None of those delicious scandals would have been printed in Saint Petersburg. Suddenly her instincts rather than her eye caught a small column of print on page 6. It read that a "James Baxter had been killed on route 95 as he headed home to Philadelphia after a business and vacation trip to Boston." His car had been hit and pushed off the road in the darkness. Baxter had died in the ambulance. Police were still looking for the car or truck that had caused the accident. Baxter worked for a computer company in Merion, Pennsylvania, where he was, according to the president, "the star among our employees." The victim had no known survivors." *Thank God he's gone,* she sniffed. *He wasn't an officer; maybe a stringer who knew too much. I didn't like him, probably the Washington resident was unhappy with him. Krushkin must have given the OK.*

ON HER NEXT TRIP to Boston, Jilly went straight to Mayfield's and waited in the unused front office. An older woman dressed for rain emerged from the inner sanctum and left quietly. Jillian added the woman to her list of concerns about Mayfield. This innocent grandmother in search of additions to her pension could very easily have dropped a bug. Mayfield had become so accustomed to his cover business that the possibility of a visitor's dropping a listening device with a hundred-meter range had disappeared from his unwritten list of precautions. She was sure that Jerry hadn't looked under the cushions of his waiting room sofa for decades.

Once again, she silently directed Jerry to remove the SIM card from his phone. "Jilly, the Center is disappointed that you've come up with nothing so far." He was delighted to try and disable her before she rankled him.

"Show me the message, Jerry. You can't can you?"

"You know I destroy communications as soon as I decipher them."

"Jerry, you are not my boss for this assignment. I am not your fucking pupil. My progress is none of your fucking business. You supply money, supplies, and communications. Running an agent or getting inside a target is beyond your reach.

You know it. I know it. And the directorate knows it.

"You are close to retirement. You want to fall off a boat en route to Europe, for your body never to be recovered? Your wife will have enough money to do ok for herself, and you both will be happier apart. You will surface in Tomsk and end up with a small dacha, a very small dacha, on the Black Sea. One day, you will end up in a rest home where the Ukrainian nurses, whom you want to screw but can't, will bring you toilet paper and tea. After a few years you will be brought into the Todtzimmer, your plug will be pulled, and that will be that.

"But you only get all that if you don't compromise this operation. If you botch it for me, the directorate might just decide to leave you here to get arrested and jailed forever with no chance of a swap. You are too trivial for that. I will be gone by then. I haven't seen any evidence they want to send me home. I am too close to pay dirt. So fuck off. Give me money and more of those new pills that keep me awake for seventy-two hours. I cached the others.

"And if you could focus on the mission, Jerry, I could use some help." Mayfield leaned back and smiled. "I heard gossip that some people on Nantucket wonder if I have relatives or a birthplace they recognize. I want to cut off suspicion before it grows. I want two relatives to visit me from Canada, stay a few days with me on the island, and send me cards and letters at Christmas. You know the drill. Have the relatives come as soon as possible, and don't forget to brief me on their backstory and how well they know me. Simple enough for you?"

"Of course, Jilly. Anything for the success of this mission. I should have an answer for you by Tuesday. You have an appointment for a small job that afternoon. It's small now. Could get much larger."

"Get off your ass, Jerry. That's all I ask." Jilly put her SIM card back into her phone, closed the door, and walked the three flights down to Dartmouth Street.

Harry Black had been right. Jilly and her earlier life remained a mystery. Killing him had not changed that. No one knew where Jillian came from, had seen her relatives, or knew her classmates. Jilly couldn't join conversations about their childrens' futures. Especially emboldened were parents who had seen their children enter the most elite of the elite colleges. She had toured Harvard and MIT for professional reasons and had concluded nothing. She also needed an alma mater and to know people who had become doctors, lawyers, artists, composers, and partners in hedge funds.

Name-dropping always popped up during a lengthy conversation or dinner, while Jilly played the sophisticated tourist and lover of the High Baroque. When pressed, she rattled off the names of towns and cathedrals that few knew. She wanted more of a story and couldn't believe that creating a fuller background for her had not been on anyone's list. *You don't send someone into a tight community with deep roots without being aware of how its denizens behave. The chief and English House were good, but not that good. How blind were they?*

A FEW MONTHS after Harry's untimely death, Jillian brightened up and broke out of the tight social circle that had supported her in the turmoil that followed Harry's death. She bought better food at the Stop and Shop, wore trendier clothes, and resumed socializing. She had her window frames painted, the door knocker polished, and cleaned up the yards. Manuel sensed that something out of the ordinary was about to happen.

Jillian let it known in a soft but proud voice that her uncle John Stafford MacGillvary and his wife Ruth would be visiting from western Canada. Jillian went aglow when the day of their arrival approached. She'd been sent background pictures and biographical information so they could converse publicly, but Mayfield had done his usual barely competent job when he sent Jilly coded details about them and how they should be treated. His last counsel was the most relevant: "Remember, you haven't seen them for years because you left and absconded to the flesh pots of Europe."

The news of their expected arrival made it to the tennis club. "I suppose we'll have to give them a drink. Do they drink, or do they belong to a sect that abhors pleasure?"

"I don't think they can go out on a boat. Wouldn't be safe."

"What if pods of nieces, nephews, and baggage follow?"

"What if they are unsuitable?"

"What happens if we don't like them?"

They were easily picked out on the ferry—she with mincing steps, he grasping the rail with a mottled right hand. At the gangway's foot, the three hugged and blocked other passengers from debarking until Jilly pulled the family reunion to a less crowded spot. Invitations soon arrived for the MacGillvarys, who appeared listless and rumpled but apparently harmless in the view of their first observers.

Jilly took her guests' bags and put them in the second bedroom. Mrs. MacGillvary's was small and light. It carried a nightgown, robe, and cosmetics. She arrived wearing a dark green dress and wore it throughout her stay. Her husband, they had married in Calgary, wore a checked shirt and a dark blue jacket that had seen many summers. His trousers were dark, and it seemed impossible to discern if he had brought a second pair. Neither brought a bathing suit. This breach of holiday necessity further established them in the islanders' minds as explorers from a distant planet.

Jilly looked out the window to see if a neighbor might crash the welcome. She turned the TV on a bit too loud. No one arrived. Jilly wrote on a yellow pad: "No compromising talk here—not swept. I searched as best I could. Everything is clean as far as I know. Remove SIM cards. We can speak, but only in English. How was the trip?"

"It went without incident. We got a hurry-up call to visit you but no materials of any kind, just who we were and how we were related to you. Our neighbors accepted that as reason for our brief holiday in the States. We bought our tickets to Montreal with cash at a small station outside Winnipeg. We rented a car from a cut-rate dealer who took cash. We paid for the motel in cash. A camera caught us at the border, but we had large sunglasses and hats. We didn't go through Logan, too many cameras, police, and drug-sniffing dogs. The bus from Boston was good cover. We used cash, but there were cameras at the ticket and boarding lines. We had to use credit cards for the ferry. And there were cameras there, too. We had changed coats and hats before we boarded. What bothered us most was everybody taking pictures of everybody else. We tried to avoid being in the backgrounds, but I'm sure someone caught us. So far, we've eaten at small restaurants and paid cash. MacGillvary is our passport name, not our name where we live in Canada. We have a cutout mailbox under MacGillvary, and you can send a Christmas card, which will be reciprocated, there. After we return home, we will send you half-a-dozen cards and notes from long-lost cousins in western Canada who are delighted that you have turned up. All in all, no trouble. We are not armed, though we have a pocket knife. We were told the affair was dry."

"I am in a safe situation here and probably good in Boston and Cambridge. I work alone on a single target. My drop and notional employer in Boston is middling incompetent. I don't think he's being watched, but his best days are behind him. I am very careful when I speak with him. You will never meet him or use him on this trip. So far, no loose ends have turned up. There is a nosey FBI agent on the island, not dangerous so far, but you never know." The MacGillvarys said nothing. They all went out the back door and continued discussions of the safety precautions.

Invitations for her guests arrived from Jilly's friends, acquaintances, and the not so few who craved local knowledge of whatever kind. The dinners were flat and repetitious in every detail. And those meals seemed to be all the locals needed. There was little interest in trying to find out more about this aunt and uncle. An older man, a local court judge, lived a few hundred yards from Jilly's house. He had abstained from neighborly formalities by design, and after a few years, no one bothered with him. He was known to drink beyond the limits his body chemistry had set, and Jilly had twice seen him fall as he groped for the morning newspaper. Late one evening when the summer sun had not yet set, Jilly's arrival home with her guests had prompted the judge's inspection of this singular visitation. He twisted his neck further than its anatomical restraints allowed, and in reentering his house, he failed to grasp the handrail. There was a fall and a sluggish rise before he turned the handle on a reluctant door and headed for bed. The judge's reconnaissance had been cursory and tepid. No other was seen.

Jilly's guests made her cringe by forgetting to be careful and dropping a word in Russian from time to time. It was enough for her to figure out that they were either White Russian or Ukrainian. Their table manners were correct, their conversation pleasant but dull, and it was apparent that they were not university graduates. Their knowledge of Canadian politics was scanty but thoughtful on the issues of immigration and wheat prices. Both needed help opening and consuming lobsters. The MacGillvarys did not entertain Jilly at dinner or lunch, claiming fatigue from the excitement of dealing with so enjoyable a vacation in a place that everyone spoke about but no one in their part of Canada had ever visited.

The appraisals did not end with their departure. "He looked quite a bit like Jilly, but she didn't. I suppose he is the blood relative."

"I suggested a walk around the Great Mill, but she claimed she left her walking shoes at home. That seemed illogical to me. Why travel if you can't walk?"

"Jilly is such an interesting person, makes friends everywhere, and has that Boston computer business going well. But they are so dull."

"Well, yes, but they are old and had a long trip. She did seem to know different teas. I suppose that is the Canadian in her."

"I think there's a bit of money there, but not too much. They mentioned only a daughter and her two children. Will probably all go to them. Jilly is a distant relative who was only his brother's ward. Wards don't even have to be relatives. Maybe the resemblance is just coincidence. I don't know, sounds like a complicated situation. More there than meets the eye, I'll bet. It'll all play out."

"They were nice enough, and they sent their bread and butter notes on very good stationery. Maybe they'll come back."

Jilly took pains not to disrupt the social balance of the group of which she had by the tacit agreement of its members become an accepted arrival. The dull MacGillvary's visit thickened her already reasonable legend. Charlie Banks took an interest in her to the extent of giving her his business account. He seemed always to be there when introductions were to be made. His velvety manners had the odd effect of calming Jilly as she made the acquaintance of new friends who spoke only English. They had an unspoken arrangement whereby if one looked at the other a nano second beyond the normal, they would find a secluded corner and talk.

CHAPTER 22

Manuelito

MANUEL AND HIS SON walked solemnly to the back door. Manuel carried his hat in both hands. Jilly came to the door before he knocked. "Manuel, how are you? Do you need something?" He seldom came to the door. The garage was his domain, and he had made clear to Jilly that he ruled that tiny wooden building. Jilly never broke the diaphanous bond that permitted him to use, lend, or appropriate, within reason and custom, whatever of Jilly's property he found necessary. Jilly had learned not to show surprise when she saw her bag of car tools sitting beside someone else's car miles from her driveway.

Manuel did excellent work. During the last hot season, he had kept the edgings around the lawn and the few surviving flowerbeds trimmed to perfection. He maintained her old car, bicycle, and her mower in perfect condition, often with tools, fluids, and God knew what else that were not hers. In any case, Jonah Coffin kept a weather eye out for undue changes in ownership or excessive use of tools and equipment scattered around the neighborhood. A word from Jonah, and one or two wrenches or a gallon of engine oil reappeared.

Jilly invited them into her kitchen. "Tea?" Manuel almost bowed and said no in a slow drawl. "Senhora Jilly, I have a request. My son Manuelito is growing up, and it is time for him to work. My family has, I hope, always satisfied you. Unlike others, we do not tell you we have worked longer than we have, and we have not taken your goods for sale in the village."

Manuel, you may be poor, she thought, *but you have a bag full of linguistic tricks to help you survive.*

"If it is possible, Senhora Jilly, Manuelito would like to work for you as my helper. He can do many things already, and I will teach him the rest. The grass will soon grow high. He likes you, Senhora, and when I am away or very busy he will do the simple things like mowing." Jilly mused that he must have rehearsed his little speech like the faux briefings she had to give at Yasenevo. Manuel kept neither a smiling nor a stern look on Jilly. Manuelito's face bent in prayerful repose. She couldn't tell if he wanted to work or was being forced away from boyhood. She wondered why Manuelito did not fulfill his apprenticeship for life aboard the fishing boats that had brought his family to the region centuries ago.

"Manuel, let me figure out if I have enough money to pay Manuelito extra. I am not rich like some on the lane. I know Manuelito is a very nice boy and that you have taught him to be honest." Manuel nodded slightly. Jilly edged to the door. The clever old coot had caught her out, and she had to show some sign of seniority over her helpers, neighborhood spies, caretakers, car mechanics, and tall trees in the wind. Suddenly she had acquired an adolescent boy to supervise.

CHAPTER 23

32

Jilly took an early flight to Logan. She had the odd feeling that she had returned home. Ingraham's office and Pinckney Street had become her nests when she left the serenity of the island. In her meticulous preparation for the Boston assignment, she had studied old maps and new satellite photos, but they did not divulge smell. They did not show the smog that on some days pained her nose. They did not convey the almost ecstatic feel of the island's salt air on a late winter day.

The chill had lifted by midmorning. The snow had melted weeks ago. Jilly walked through the Public Gardens on her favorite path. She loved that fifty-acre patch of Boston, even the chain fences that warned walkers off the grass without a sign and or menacing guards. She had come to know its trees and shrubs and patches of grass. It was near spring, and they had become friends, and had she been asked, she could have named most of them.

She sensed the different kinds of walkers and crowds who strolled or rushed at every waking hour. It was not a matter of blending in with them. She was one of them. She saw the crowd as a conglomeration of bytes, the misplacing of any of which triggered an alarm. She fancied she could detect surveillance as well as if someone had brought an extra guest to dinner.

This day promised a rare cloudless splendor until a danger signal passed through her brain. At first she could not decipher it. Then she saw 32's face. Their eyes met. He came toward her on an opposite path. She shuddered to a stop and scanned for a tail. She switched paths so that she could walk directly behind him. After five minutes, she saw no discordant eyes watching either one of them. One of her class's few sullen dummies, 32 was hatless and wore a cheap raincoat. His thinning hair swept over his broad brow. His skin was sallow, his eyes dull. He walked languidly with his mouth half open. Far from collecting secrets of state, he looked as though he had given up on life. He was dangerous.

At Yasenevo, he had proclaimed to anyone within ear shot that he was a true son of the working classes with little formal education. Everyone knew that he was the inept son of a Rostov party hack and had gotten admission to the Sluzhba through the apparat. She had by chance eaten with him in the dining hall occasionally. He had impaired table manners. He slurped his soup and harpooned small vegetables as if enemies of the state. Classmates stopped eating to watch him spear a small pickle.

Jilly got behind him and gradually came up to his back. "Keep on walking. Do not brush by me or turn around. If you speak a word of Russian, I will kill you here. I have a ricin needle. What the fuck are you doing on my turf, you slimy son of a bitch? Don't answer! You know that black officers are not supposed to work within a hundred miles of each other. If you compromise me, I will find you and kill you. He almost looked behind himself but stopped. Here is what you are going to do: keep walking up Boylston Street. Do you know street names here?"

"Yes, 75." Whatever stolid resolve he had at the day's beginning evaporated.

She ran out of breath and paused. "Go right and walk until you get to Boylston Street. Use the strict security procedures for foreign streets. Do you remember what that means?"

"Yes, 75. We all knew what a bitch you were after 6 drowned."

"You will worse than drown if you fuck me up. Meet me at 12:30 at the left-hand lion at the bottom of the steps to the public library. If you are clean, hold a copy of the Boston Globe in your left hand. If you fail to follow these instructions, I will find you and cut you. Larynx, heart, dick. Shall I go on?"

"I know I'm clean," he simpered.

"Speed up your walk so that the distance between us increases, and God help you if you don't make the meet. After you see me, and we are as clean as your fuckup permits, go to South Station and take the next train to New York. Do not make phone calls or drop paper or make signals like unbuttoning your coat. I will watch you. Once aboard the train, clean yourself if you remember how and take the next train to Philadelphia. I assume that the poor soul who employs you will have taught you what to do next. Tell your boss to keep you two-hundred miles from my area of operations. If he or she compromises me, I will take the proper measures."

32 translated the phrase into Russian and realized Jillian's meaning.

"Now repeat the instructions I gave you, comma by comma." He did, with despair and hatred. Jilly recalled the pointed instruction that she, as a singleton, was responsible for the operation. Others' mistakes on the ground were her problem, not the Center's. A breeze came off Beacon Hill and did little to dry the moisture on her forehead.

Once he took off as instructed, Jilly called Jerry at his office and told him she'd be late but would return about three.

"Well, I hope that you got that nice account I put you onto in Malden."

What an ass! "That and more, Jerry." She turned right onto Arlington Street and watched as 32 headed toward Copley Square. The strong forward step demanded at the school had somehow gotten lost, and 32 seemed to ooze up the sidewalk rather than walk.

JILLY SAUNTERED up Newbury Street looking into every third window. She crossed and then turned right on Exeter and headed toward the river and the esplanade. She cleaned herself carefully. She hated even the idea of face-to-face meetings and brush contacts. The former always turned into arguments. The latter were simply dangerous. Both were strictly forbidden in the orders she had memorized at English House. Jilly was too close to success to allow such tomfoolery. All intelligence operations end in entropy. Was this boob a downward link to a failed end? She had to discover what he was doing near her in Boston. Was he watching her? Had he sold out to work for the Bureau or the London oligarchs? Or was he paying a part in someone else's mission? If the latter, why was he not told to avoid Boston?

She twisted back toward Copley Square and saw him standing at the bottom of the library steps. A copy of the Boston Globe was tucked under his left arm. "OK, 32, what the fuck are you doing here? Who are you working for? If it's not the First Directorate, I will kill you with the poison in my right hand right now."

"It's legitimate, 75. I work for Krushkin, just like you. I live in Philadelphia and the nachalnika there needed some fast courier work to an agent here who doesn't have comms. I am still loyal."

"You are still stupid"

"Think what you want. I am here under orders. If you hurt me or blow me, repercussions will follow, unpleasant repercussions."

"Don't threaten me, you pile of goat excrement. Here is what you will do. You will walk to South Station now. You will buy a ticket to Philadelphia. The Red Train leaves hourly. I will follow you at a distance, but I will always see you, and I will watch you board. You will remain on the train until Philadelphia. Do not return to Boston for as long as I am assigned here. If you do you, you will not walk again. Tell that to whoever sent you. Do you understand?"

"Yes, 75. You are a perfect bitch and the Center will hear of this."

"Tell them the whole story and what I promised will happen to you if I see you again," Jilly replied. A hundred yards apart, they walked solemnly to South Station. 32 boarded the 3:00 pm train for New York and points south. Jilly waited until the last car was out of sight, took a cab, and stopped two blocks from Jerry's office.

BETTER NOT TELL him, Jilly thought. He might be part of it. She wondered how her threats to 32 would redound to her if, in fact, 32 ever told the Center. He was such a weakling he would probably concoct a phony story that he had detected surveillance and could not deliver his package. His boss in Philadelphia would write him up as gutless and send someone else.

Jilly was frightened that it had given her so much pleasure to instill fear in a man trained as she had been. She had watched him as he walked by the Hancock Building, where she had read that glass had fallen from faulty windows when it was being built. She half hoped a piece would skip through the air and land on 32.

She took the creaky elevator to the third floor, walked down the ancient seasick-green corridor, and entered Jerry's suite. He had a client, so she waited in the outer office where Jerry's oft-promised, but never hired, secretary would have sat. The door opened. Jerry and a badly dressed woman of forty or so appeared and said goodbye. Jerry locked the door and loosened his tie. She stood by the couch, removed her clothes, and lay down. They had decided that sex might relax the tension that had frayed their relationship. Jerry hadn't fucked a Russian woman in years, Jilly thought, and it might remind him of home and keep his loyalties where they belonged. Jerry stripped, and they had seven minutes of mindless, garlic scented sex that Jilly reminded herself was banal, brittle, brusque, and boring. They dressed.

She paused and wrote on a pad: "Sweep Jerry? Jerry do you ever sweep this office?"

"Yeah, I have an outsider from a security firm come in every month. I tell her that I have confidential talks here. She believes me." Jerry asked, "Why, any security problems?"

"No, I always take the usual precautions. This time I took the ferry to Hyannis and the bus here."

"Well, I suppose the simplest way is the best way."

"Anything from the Center?"

"No, only the usual hurry-up request for progress reports, progress of which I suppose you've had little. Remember, you have a one-target job, a one-recruiting job, a one-theft job, and you live damn well."

The moral victory she had gained over 32 gave her unusual confidence about handling Mayfield. "Philip James Ingraham has an open mouth and the hook dangles near. I get good jobs with the right people on the island. I have built an exceptionally good cover. Even your pathetic contracts add a little to the pot. I have no tedious lawsuits, license problems, or bothersome entanglements that might interfere with the job. I have one target.

"The take, when it gets taken from my about-to-be friend Professor Ingraham and his laboratory, will go onto the thumb drives I give you to send back to the Center. Nothing in my house compromises me. It's very simple. Leave me alone, and the contents of Phil's computer will soon be ours," she replied with one breath in a firm, imperious tone that she hoped would trump Jerry's leaden bullying.

He went to his safe, opened it, and handed Jilly ten-thousand dollars in well-used bills. "More eighteenth-century furniture for your guests to admire?"

She answered, "Don't you have a little stashed away after skimming the Center all these years, Jerry? Don't tell me a few bills never stuck to your sweaty fingers?"

The attack stung. "Jilly, we are on the same team," he answered. "I want to ensure that you buy your treasures in cash from merchants who don't have all-seeing cameras." They went over Jilly's communications signals and emergency exfiltration schedule. Clandestine communications to and from the island were awkward. A coded call from

Jerry about contracts and new accounts was the only way she got new directions she didn't want. Chalk signs on the Safeway parking lot's posts alerted her to call him. She always wondered who made those damn chalk marks.

CHAPTER 24

Just Plain Luke

JILLY HAD ENDURED many often painful interrogations from a mock FBI agent at Yasenevo. The chief instructor had once been jailed and harshly questioned, first by Virginia State Troopers and then by the FBI. They accused him of being a courier for the Washington residentura. They found nothing incriminating in his car or apartment because he had stopped at a gas station, gone to the men's room, and flushed his papers. They disintegrated upon contact with water, and he emerged clean from there and the interrogation. A few months later, after he saw no trailers, he left the country. Jilly knew that Bob Horan would call again. Trouble was, she did not know his target.

THE CALL CAME after a decent interval. "Hi, Jilly, this is Bob Horan. How are you?"

"What can I do for you?"

"It's bicycle weather, top-down weather." His sounded unnecessarily charming. "Could you drop down to the office today? The problem we discussed before has gotten bigger."

"Sure Bob. After lunch."

"Perfect." They hung up with no further strained pleasantries. She assumed Horan had sketched a floor plan of her house after his visit and would have the place searched while she was away. It was a small house. There was nothing on her desk top, laptop, or tablet that would point to anything but a growing small business with diverse clients on both the island and the mainland. They would copy her data, but they wouldn't remove the drives without a warrant. She could not get outraged and would not ask for a lawyer because this meeting was something whose true purpose she was not supposed to understand. She occasionally had trouble peeing because a trainer at Yasenevo had landed a blow to her kidney when she believed that the exercise interrogation was finished. The memory and the pain stayed with her. But now, she was clueless as to Horan's purpose,

It was hot bicycling to Horan's. She had dressed like an islander, in the shorts, good shirt with rolled up sleeves, and sockless mocs that informal meetings allowed. At the office, a tall and unattractive man a in coat and tie stood beside Horan. No one on the island wore a coat except on Saturday nights at the tennis club.

"Did I tell you a colleague was visiting? I barely know how to send my mother an email, but Luke here knows more about your side of things and will better understand anything you tell us. He's my interpretor to your world, I guess you could say. Luke, meet Jillian Carlson, our local computer whiz. I can't pronounce Luke's last name. It's Polish. Everyone calls him Just Plain Luke." Jilly immediately christened him Lothar after an extremely unpleasant instructor at Yasenevo.

Luke extended a freakishly large hand and rumbled, "Happy to meet you, Jillian, if I may call you that." He surely is a Lothar, she thought. His bulbous eyes remained open to their maximum diameter as though they had been glued. His hair crept down to his eyes, obscured the bridge of his nose, and almost impaired his vision. They showed a level of disappointment close to anger. She could not tell if this was because his children had bad grades or because he viewed Jilly as a convicted criminal condemned forever to a super-max prison.

"Let's use the conference room." Horan directed them into a small space with a long table and eight chairs. Horan almost grudgingly let Jillian enter first. The one window, high on the wall, gave little light. All told, the banal brown room was one step away from a similarly used space in Yasenevo.

"The hacking problem has widened and deepened. It continues, apparently randomly, but it's hitting more people and is, Luke tells me, much more sophisticated than I understood. We have told the very rich and super rich on the island to secure their files and reports. They have their own expensive safeguards on the mainland, but Luke here thinks that none of the defenses the local cable provider use are impervious to the sophisticated intrusions he has picked up. We've found one commonality among the people affected. Before you got here, people went off-island for help setting up equipment and software, and it seems that many of the hacked accounts had links to techs recommended by Jerry Mayfield. You use him too, don't you?"

"Yes, he gotten me good work, though he takes more than his pound of flesh from any account he sends my way. He has a sweet deal. He sits, I do the work. He canvasses State Street and the medical profession for new accounts. But as far as I can tell, he's always square with me. My clients pay him the contracted fees, and he clears my account at the end of the month. He's never slow or short. It would be hard to hide if he were charging them more than he tells me."

Luke spoke up: "Did you ever meet any of his other clients? Do you have a grasp of how he does business or who his friends are?"

"I have seen a few middle-aged women at his office. One came out as I entered last time I was there, and one came in as I left. Usually nobody but me is there. He has no secretary. Too cheap, I think. Oh, and one time there was a geeky young guy with a shoulder bag and too much hair. You could pick him out as a graduate student from a mile away. My sense is that Mayfield spends most of his time cold-calling prospective clients."

"How did you learn programming, Jillian" Jilly recognized the tone of one professional speaking to another in the slight Slavic born emphasis at the end of a sentence. "My grandparents were my guardians. When they died within a few months of each other, I found myself with an inheritance. I picked up and went to Europe. I visited parks and museums in Germany and the Baltics, but I liked sailing and landed in Copenhagen. I wasn't good enough, though, couldn't sail competitively. I was using money pretty fast, and as I told Bob, I went to the Copenhagen Institute. I was looking for a career that would keep me out of corporate life and office politics. And it has. Best decision of my life."

Just Plain Luke and Horan gave simultaneous nods. Luke asked Jilly questions about computers and software whose answers she knew but did not give up. His nose was so large that when he leaned forward, his face seemed to fill the room. Horan bought her story, she concluded. If Luke wanted to, he would have no trouble checking Jilly's educational background, something a Lothar would certainly do.

Jilly half hoped that he would. A Jillian Carlson had entered and graduated from Copenhagen Institute with an excellent record. She had completed her practicum at a local hotel. Her records existed. Still, if Mayfield had been fingered, Jilly would not be able to telephone or visit him. She had to report the FBI interview and her concerns to the Center. That was doctrine, and she had procedures for handling it. As they got up to leave, Luke leaned over in a conspiratorial stance and asked, "Have you ever heard of the Kozodoy 12 Algorithm, Jilly?"

Ha! Jilly thought. Kozodoy was one of her father's friends, and she had served him all those Sunday lunches. "I have heard of it from some instructors in Copenhagen, but it's way over my head." Again, two nods of acceptance. Luke's hair flopped irregularly when he moved. *My God. He's wearing a toupee. Not only is he a Lothar, but he's a hairless Lothar.*

Jilly left the room first, walking through the outer office into the pleasant warmth and brilliant sunshine that Nantucket provides in spring and summer. The secretary did not look up. Jilly headed for the ice cream store and bought a strawberry cone. The Belgian waffle was too heavy and disguised the flavor of the ice cream. Mikoyan, the Armenian, had brought ice cream to Russia, Jilly remembered, but not even the shop on Nevski Prospect produced anything as good as the scoop in her hand.

HORAN AND LUKE sat with their unfinished reports. Horan leaned back in the creaky government chair, looked at the wall, and mumbled, "I dunno."

"Me neither, Bob."

THE CLEVERNESS of Krushkin's plan was as clear to Jilly as it might be to the FBI. No materiel except a thumb drive had to be transported out of the country. Jilly didn't have to search for codes, designs, or plans as her predecessors had in the last century. She had only to copy data which she herself did not understand. She also had to stay clean. This might be nothing; Jilly had no idea how many other computer hacks were being interviewed or even put under surveillance. The FBI had her picture, her voice and finger prints, possibly her DNA from a hair brush in her bathroom. It had thin sketch of how she came to Nantucket. Her only vulnerability lay with blunders Mayfield might make and the discovery of his links to the Sluzhba. She gave her unseen intruders enough time to search, to copy, and to plant a listening device, probably in her bedroom.

Her bicycle was still locked in the rack outside the supermarket, and she pedaled home quickly to avoid the afternoon traffic. At the house, she caught the lingering scent of the powder from the rubber gloves Horan's intruders had used when copying her hard drive. The knives in her cutlery drawer had been moved. She had left a shirt draped over her desktop computer as if she had left in a hurry and not put it away. Underneath the placket to which a button was sewn, the dangling threads were not as she had left them. Pretty good, she thought, but not quite top drawer. Lothar had come up with nothing. Jilly was certain of that, because there was nothing to find. Still, Jillian Augusta Carlson was a person of interest to the US government.

CHAPTER 25

The Gardner Museum

THE WOMAN IN the seat opposite ate her breakfast from a plastic container. A poorly masked hunger overrode her concern for stains and crumbs. Toast and eggs disappeared in short minutes. Since Yasenevo Jilly had failed to organize a proper breakfast. Hardship, cold and fatigue induced the staff there to lay on a heavy breakfast of kasha, fruit, bread and cheese. Sleepiness and trepidation about the day's miseries limited conversation. Jilly yearned for the kasha and berries of her training days and the mugs of tea and thick slices of black bread that Olga Filipova prepared in her father's kitchen; but prudence kept her distant from the shops in Boston that held meager supplies of Russian groceries. For the island's colder mornings, she bought Irish oatmeal as a pale substitute. Horan might be impressed, she grumbled to herself.

AFTER AN APPOINTMENT at a four-doctor practice whose investment accounts had become so muddled that an inquirer would discover a commercial block in Malden was by chance mortgaged to a major drug company in Switzerland, Jilly left for the subway. In time, she imposed order on these brilliant men's affairs so they could sustain examination from the Internal Revenue Service, an event that in their case was sure to happen.

All her contractors asked her the same question: "Jilly, you can't spend all you time sitting in front of a keyboard. How do you spend the rest of your days?" These questions were the stuff either of honest curiosity or the occasional opening lines of a flirtation. Jilly denied to her contractors that computers filled her life and boasted that art held sway over men, alcohol, and drugs. Such chitchat deflected the burgeoning ardor of those few who considered a night away from family as a perquisite of profit from successful drug trafficking, tax evasion, or passing encoded betting information to and from Las Vegas. He probably didn't know much about germ warfare.

JILLY VISITED the Gardner Museum, not her first trip, and made her way up the stairs to the blank space on the wall from which the pictures had been removed many years before. Finally, he was there. Standing before the empty space, apparently in a state of meditation, was an early middle-aged man dressed in a tweed coat and dark pants. He had graying hair, a slight stoop, but an almost unlined face. Philip Ingraham, Jilly's purpose in her life, turned toward her. *Will he turn back? All that training and mud. All those blisters and the Dagestani on Berezon Island, all wasted unless a middle-aged professor likes my smile, my chest, and my legs.* Jilly edged beside Ingraham and let a moment pass before she spoke. "I miss the Vermeer most. The musicians sent shivers down my spine." He looked at her and said nothing. He turned away and surveyed her before his eyes centered on the blank spaces.

"The Rembrandt was my father's favorite. Once he saw it, he never recovered. I don't think that anyone could love it more. I hope the person who has it now loves it half as much."

"I can't figure if the theft came from a love of the paintings or from the satisfaction of having pulled off what so far is the perfect robbery. Or maybe the person who hangs it now has a sociopathetic side to him that gloats because he can see it morning, noon, and night, but no one else can"

"Who says it's a him? Maybe it's a she who wanted a peculiar sort of revenge on Mrs. Gardener for having acquired the paintings and kept them in her name in a building named after her. Or maybe she just loves them."

"I'm Jillian Carlson, by the way. Women don't steal art. Some man or a group of men or a hidden exhibition run by men in a dark cave has these paintings."

"Philip Ingraham."

Jillian's ire was genuine, and she continued her tear without even nodding in acknowledgement. "I am certain that the pictures have each gone their separate ways. Together they were too hot to handle. Imagine storing them! You'd need the kind of armed guard the Gardener should have had.

"I'm worried the crooks will mistreat the paintings or sell them to someone who won't take proper care of them. Maybe the robber wanted to be a hero to himself, to congratulate himself every day as he looked at them. I think that he purrs to himself. Mutters, 'I did it and no one else has come close to such a masterful job.'"

"I seem to have started you on your favorite subject of stealing treasures that have remained hidden for decades. I understand, Ms. Carlson. The robbery still exasperates me, and I have lived in this city for a very long time. Do you live around here?"

"No, Mr. Ingraham. I work partly on Nantucket where I live, and I have some accounts in Boston and Cambridge."

"You're in sales?"

"No, computer assistance."

"I started you on a subject that you seem passionate about. Let's have a cup of tea to continue the argument." They went to the café sat at a table away from others. "Is there much work for you on Nantucket? Or is the lack why you're here? Other than the fine arts, of course."

"I chose Nantucket because I love to sail, like good food, and wanted a place of my own where I can escape from the city. I have to come to town, though, as you guessed, to pick up work to ferry back to the island. And you?"

"I do research. On bugs and what they can do to humanity. I have very competent associates who perform what I call the *day work*, the stuff that an ordinary PhD can finish within a few years.

"Let me explain. Years ago I wrote and published a seminal article that set me above the other journeymen in the field. I got tenure and some grant money. I do the *night work*. I connect their unconnected dots and some dots of my own that I didn't know existed.

"I try to reach conclusions nobody else has unearthed yet or even knew existed, like Rembrandt. The science I do is a matter of creation rather than experimentation. Even if I attach a "Memo of Methods" to my work, no one will be able to replicate it. I am not building on anyone else's research because it is new and unique."

"I get it. I am not a nerd or a science geek, but I understand what you've explained. I think. I never took an advanced degree. I get hired less because of my computer skills and more because I know business practices fairly well and can help with both American business law and Common Market protocols. I work with what I can see or what my employers tell me."

"And how does a computer analyst pick all that up? Or did business come first and algorithms second?"

"I guess you could say they arrived together. I had spent a few years in Europe doing nothing, and then when I began to run out of money, I went back to school at the Computer Institute in Copenhagen." Jilly leaned forward to make her point. "I learned computing from very good teachers. But I also worked at a Copenhagen hotel. It was insignificant as hotels go, but they had to fill out all the forms for the bureaucrats in Brussels, the stuff that the European Union demands. I learned the credit-card part of the business, too."

"Ever get to Bruges? It's one of the most beautiful places in Europe. It makes you feel good to be a human being."

"No, my boyfriend at the time chose to visit all things Baroque in Southern Germany. I will rectify that mistake next time I'm over."

Ingraham leaned forward, more to examine Jilly's face than to catch her every word. "I love my work, but I would rather spend my time at the museum. Even when some of my favorite canvases have gone missing."

"I will sleep on your notion about female robbers. But it's much too fanciful. It simply couldn't happen."

"Maybe so, but I think that women have hungers and capacities that even the philosophers don't know." Jillian smiled at the badly mauled quote more because it was stolen than for its truth.

"I must go, Philip. It has been a pleasure meeting you."

"Likewise. I make it a point to visit here once a week. Perhaps we might synchronize our visits. Perhaps a lunch afterwards."

"Don't know what day I'll be in town. Give me your number, and I'll ring you up." He did. "Can I give you a lift?'

"Thanks, but I have an appointment nearby. It's a nice walk."

PROFESSOR PHILIP FRANCIS INGRAHAM pushed the ignition button, wondering if she was a woman of bending ecstasy or one who would prattle on upright about the Jesuitical exaggerations of the High Baroque. *Never been to Bruges? My God!*

Jilly passed the Medical School and walked down Avenue Louis Pasteur past Latin School. *Did I get him, or did I put him off? God, I wish Helga had taken me to Bruges. It was only a little way off our route. He doesn't quite meet the standards of a Petersburg Sunday lunch, but he is civilized.* She picked up work on Huntington Avenue from a secretary whose boss claimed a phone call prevented their talking. Jilly forgave his rudeness—he paid her on time. She took the bus to Hyannis and the last ferry to the island. She shoved her raincoat and laptop in the front straw basket and pedaled home. *Shall I dream about him tonight or not? Not a good idea.*

JILLY CALLED the number Philip Ingraham gave her. A raspy voice that was recognizably female answered. Jilly left a message that next Thursday was not good, but that the following Thursday was fine and could he call back if he was open that day. Jilly fought her excitement, found herself thinking in Russian, and tried to use her best American business language. That evening, a familiar voice left a message that a week from Thursday was fine. They could decide where to eat after they met. Olga Filipova had not taught her how to select a proper lover nor how to avoid becoming an unhappy wife. *No matter. Krushkin has chosen my paramour for me.*

CHAPTER 26

The Quotidian and the Penny Dreadfuls

SPRING HAD ARRIVED, interrupted randomly by chilling rains from the north. Jilly wore her blue Bean raincoat against nature's unpredictability. She spent half her island time working on the hospital's inventory accounts and drug licenses. The backlog would take days to unravel, put in order, and send off to the bureaucrats in Boston and Washington who sought fuel for their murky endeavors.

Much of the rest of the time she spent working for Charlie Banks, the island's best litigator, who got citizens into or out of trouble. He needed her because practicing the law effectively kept him from keeping his affairs in any semblance of good order, and he had hired a secretary rather than a law clerk. It was not clear what Mrs. Gates knew or what her quiver of skills contained. Banks knew the laws and regulations that applied to the people of Nantucket and cared to know nothing more. He was not good with numbers. How a man who managed to secure early court dates when other attorneys languished, settle complex cases out of court, and fix Jilly's traffic tickets remained a puzzle to her even after she did meticulous research into the matter.

Most of the islander's legal affairs bored her into a peculiar state of delirium that others mistook for concentration. But some cases held her interest more than an afternoon. His divorce cases, most routine, a few very juicy, took the biggest chunk of her time. From these Jilly learned tales of woe and deceit that would put Penny Dreadfuls to shame. One very proper and rich islander had a second family on the mainland, a wife, three children, and two dogs. They all lived in a fine house with a garden. His name appeared on the children's birth certificates.

When the second wife died prematurely, his name appeared on critical documents. Those handling her estate tried to keep the matter as quiet as possible, but the island wife discovered her husband's other life and diminished his considerable wealth by half. He managed to take care of his mainland children nonetheless, and they all went to private schools and fine colleges.

Then there was the man with wives on the island, in Boston, and in Palm Beach. Complicating the situation was that the wife in Palm Beach found herself married at the same time to a gentleman in her neighborhood who was living under an alias while hiding his foreign citizenship with a professionally forged US passport. The passport was so well done the FBI lab was studying it an effort to discover its fabricator.

On the way home, she walked by the supermarket parking lot and scanned the post for a message. One white chalk mark meant she should visit her contact on the next trip to Boston. Two marks on successive poles meant come immediately, and three meant execute the emergency exfiltration plan and leave immediately. The person who posted the marks would not know what the marks meant, only that they should be placed exactly at the prescribed spot and immediately.

The exfiltration plan was awkward and almost impossible to execute under duress. It required her to leave for Boston on the next air or sea transport and wait in front of the Boston Athenaeum at 10½ Beacon Street for a man carrying a *New York Times* under his left arm while she watched for surveillance. Precisely fifteen minutes later, the same man would pass with the *Times* under his right arm. If Jillian had discovered the man was being tailed, she would be gone when he reappeared. The Yasenevo rules stipulated that she must formulate such a plan considering the local operational circumstances. But Jilly knew that execution of that impossibly complex choreography was impractical. She would be caught or shot or both.

CHAPTER 27

Second Lunch

THEY MET AT NOON. Jilly ensured that she arrived later than Ingraham. Her first words when she got there again addressed the empty wall. "I still love the Vermeer musicians. I went home and looked at a reproduction after we spoke. They had such a rollicking good time."

"True, but so does the person who can look at them every day." At lunch, they talked again about the robbery and who might have committed it. She wondered aloud if the crime would ever be solved and, more important, if the paintings would ever return home.

Ingraham turned the conversation. I have an odd office problem, Jilly. I hope I don't bore you. I can't explain it to my wife. My office files are a mess. My postdocs' work needs to be recorded for university records and for my grantor, a private foundation. Mrs. Cruikshank, my secretary, couldn't begin to do that and the postdocs don't dare to touch my record system. They are too frightened. They know their next job depends on me. He paused in silence as though awaiting celestial counsel and rose. "I'm afraid my worrying about all that must wait. I must get back to my lab. Why don't we have a slap-dash dinner at my flat next week? It's small, but it has a very efficient kitchen. I cook a few things well for myself. I am alone so much that I haven't learned to cook for others. I can't guarantee a splendid Nantucket lobster, but I'll think of something."

"My next job is Friday next week. I've had bachelors' cooking before, Philip. And meals prepared by women who could not cook at all but were not dissuaded from having dinner parties. Nothing you fetch up could possibly be worse than the worst I've already encountered." They rose. Philip helped with her coat and left a substantial tip for the unexciting meal. They parted outside.

He seemed to be interested both in her and her office skills, she reasoned. *I think he's a little bit afraid to make the pitch. He's afraid of rejection.* One of her instructors had advised her to "let the new pigeon propose to you. You will, in many cases have reached the point after a few meetings that recruitment is the next step. All is timing. Do not take the first step. Your prospect will propose the next move to you and let you decide if you will accept or reject."

CHAPTER 28

Dinner

THE EVENING of the dinner, Jilly arrived fifteen minutes late. She wore standard Boston drab but smiled more than the average worker in downtown. It reminded her of Petersburg in June , when everyone ventured outside, pale after the long winter. She pushed the button for the eighth floor and found Philip Ingraham waiting at the door. He hovered over her and then walked back to a small table set with decanters. "I spoke with my wine broker about a good red and a good white for a special occasion. You will taste the red later, a 1966 Talbot, but the white, he says. is unusual. It is a Riesling from the Moselle region of Germany." He handed her a glass with a gold rim. "Well, here's to us." *If all courtships featured gold rimmed glasses and good wine, this life might not be just unpredictable but educational.*

They touched glasses, and Jilly sat. If Helga had been there she would have sniffed and blown out her cheeks and gargled before rendering a long analysis of Philip's excellent white wine. Then she'd talk about its finish, the length it lingered on the tongue, and the aroma. Midway through the meal, if she weren't flirting with a table of wealthy-looking German men, she would have described the effect of the fish on the wine and vice versa.

Philip clattered about in the small kitchen and then brought out a massive slice of paté with crackers. "This paté is delicious, Philip, better than the ones I ate in Alsace."

"Glad you like it. Not often I have a dinner companion who has your taste for the unsung glories of France. Meat should be ready now." Philip turned his back, clattered even more loudly, and brought out two plates covered with filet mignon, carrots, and small potatoes. The mahogany table could seat four, but two was better. The plates were delicate and the silver was old and heavy.

Jilly had not eaten lunch and plunged into the under-cooked steak. The carrots had been boiled into tasteless mush. The potatoes were poor and hard, testifying to their brief acquaintance with boiling water. Phillip finally spoke. "I know you doubt the likelihood that the museum was robbed by women, but I have some family stories of unreported crimes probably committed by that gender. And fairly rich women at that."

"I assumed you had a spotless ancestry."

"No, not from my family, though we are a dreary and straight-forward bunch. When I was young, we had people over to tea, that being a meal in itself. In Dedham, competition grew to put on the best tea, especially around Thanksgiving and Christmas. Suddenly, my parents began to miss small pieces of cutlery. The cook and servant were saved from being fired when family friends reported the same occurrences in their houses. One or two pieces of the family's silver, probably owned for two or three generations, had disappeared. Happened randomly for three months. Nobody reported the thefts to the police because the investigations would have touched too many honest and prominent people."

Jilly rose from her chair. "Philip, you are not a boring man, but this story is boring. In a moment, when you run out of duped ancestors and felonious neighbors, you will become tongue-tied. I don't think you mean for that to happen." She stood up and took his hand, he rose from his chair, and they walked into the flat's other room. They awoke in peace. Their feet touched, but they said nothing. Philip rose, and Jilly rolled over into the warmth of his side of the bed. Both left the building at the same time, and they kissed on the sidewalk. Their fingers touched again. Philip walked to his car, and Jilly strode off.

MAYFIELD'S OUTER DOOR was open, so Jilly entered without the usual twisting demanded by the old doorknob. Mayfield looked up. "Jilly how are you? What news?" They removed their SIM cards and turned up the music channel. He moved toward the sofa.

"Sorry, Jerry, not this time, I'm monogamous."

"Aha, you found the Golden Fleece—or whatever it is called these days."

"What is the Golden Fleece?"

"I forget you a wouldn't know the symbol. I didn't either until I learned the whole story from my son while he did his homework. You have taken the first step toward a major success. And there have been no changes in communications, plans, drops, or anything else." He turned toward his old iron safe and removed a packet of assorted used and washed bills. "I will inform our superiors that you have made contact with the target and will report progress as it occurs."

"Jerry, any surveillance on you or me? Anybody else operating on my grounds?"

"None known or reported to me." Jilly hadn't removed her coat and moved to the door. She opened it and turned toward Mayfield. "You remind me of a dog that whines outside the owner's door until he gets attention instead of a boot in the ass. Fuck you." She closed the door and walked down the stairs to Dartmouth Street. It was still a bright day. She smiled at the old lady who seemed always to be toting a shopping bag toward the building across the street.

Jilly called Philip on his private number. "The Vermeer tomorrow?"

"Of course. My opinion remains the same. I have put a higher value on it in the last day or two."

"I thought you might. Tomorrow." The dissimulations inherent in seduction had vanished. Each had measured the other.

CHAPTER 29

Entrée

"Jilly, I want to be with you. I want you near me. I have a plan. Record keeping remains outside the ken of my loyal secretary. Mrs. Cruikshank is very good at tracking the politics of the department. She will trade who has tooth trouble for a senior professor who came in late and hungover. She knows who takes home boxes of paper clips and who has a bottle of vodka in the lower right-hand drawer. Most important, she knows who is applying for what grants and who serves on which committees. She knows whom every member of the senior faculty will back and to whom they are hostile. Basically, she rules her own kingdom for herself. Protecting me is a necessary side line. Sometimes I think that she thinks I work for her. There are days when she orders me about like few others I have known.

"But she refuses to learn how to use a computer beyond the simplest tasks. She claims they are instruments of the devil. I think she really believes that. And although she believes that I do the work of the Lord, she treats all else with the indifference it would deserve if not bureaucratically required for my work. In her way, she has defeated me and her job description. Foundation reports and faculty memos overwhelm her, even as she manages to protect me from departmental nonsense and people who waste my time on the phone.

"My postdocs are great in the lab but otherwise useless. They cannot keep track of the work they have very successfully completed. Right now, my office would not pass an audit from the university or from the foundation that supports my work and the flat on Pinckney. So I have a proposal. I want you to straighten out my records, update progress reports to the foundations, answer the occasional rude letter, and keep me out of trouble with the department and the university. Annual audits are coming up, and I no longer have a good assistant to do the books. Last one left six months ago, and I haven't had a chance to replace him. In the meantime, Cruikshank refuses to adhere to university requirements and instead tells the deans that I don't have the time to submit the gobbledygook they insist upon. She treated one dean with such scorn that he asked me to fire her. This can't continue until the next set of annual reports is due.

"What happens if the grant money dries up?"

"For a while, I can ride on my stature in the field. The university doesn't want me ripped away by a state school that will triple my salary. The computer companies want me to use their products, so I receive the best of their world for a penny on the dollar. Ultimately, I would have to teach more. But as long as I produce consistently good work and remain a superb grant writer, I can keep this life until I want to retire."

"And you want me to make sure there are no glitches."

"Work for me part time, whenever you are free from your other work. Sign a confidential business agreement. When the foundations understand that you don't tell tales out of school and that they have a professional keeping track of my work for them, they will sit quietly in their corners while you generate boring and unreadable reports that few will understand and none will criticize. I can hire you at a university grade that will give you two or three days a week here and sixty-thousand dollars a year."

"I am not a bag of vegetables or a case of wine, Philip. I am not a commodity like your graduate students to be bought, shared, traded, dismissed, or sold like post docs. If you trade me off, I shall become very angry."

"Never, Jilly".

"Philip do you recall that portrait of Queen Elizabeth the First? It was either by Gheeraerts or Oliver. It shows the Queen dressed in a cloak decorated with eyes and ears."

"I don't remember much from my course in nineteenth-century British history."

I'll let that one pass, dear Philip. "I am all eyes and ears if it comes to your dalliances."
He reddened. *So he can feel guilt. That's a weapon.*

CHAPTER 30

The Office

JILLY MADE THE VISIT to Ingraham's office the last of the day. All but the most devoted grad students had either left or were preparing to catch their buses to Somerville or hop on the subway to the bars of Kendall Square. Ingraham's office was spacious, but quite a bit smaller than her father's on Vasilevski Island. It had a clear view across the Charles River into Boston. He had a book-lined room with chairs, a sofa and a handsome desk. The chairs were set well back from the desk's front in order to maintain a respectful distance between petitioner and prince. No intimacies among conspirators were meant to occur here.

Plaques on the white walls attested to his scholarly achievements. Except for those listed with his ascending degrees, the institutions they named were obscure and meant to be unintelligible to the uninitiated. A letter of thanks from the president of an institution in Southhampton, England for chairing a forum surely impressed a few subordinates. The office did not offer welcome or warmth. It was a throne room. The air was glacial and indifferent to life.

Beatrice Chruikshank sat outside at a long wooden desk that had been in service for decades. She treated all visitors as threats to the disciplined tranquility of her empire. She told most callers that Professor Ingraham was in the lab when he was at his desk and advised them he had left the building when he worked in the lab. Woe betide any member of the faculty or staff, no matter how senior, who shirked what she saw as responsibilities to her lord. She despised Jilly.

Two post-doc assistants shared a smaller office but usually worked in the lab. They saw themselves as scientists who labored for a great man on his way to understanding the fundamental properties of airborne bacteria and frowned on Jilly as a mere technician. Yet they put open hostility aside because Jilly knew more than they in her one narrow field and because she was tasked with recording their progress. "Ms. Carlson, here is my weekly update" was all Jilly expected to hear beyond "could you pass the cream please" at the complicated coffee machine. She was careful because they moved silently in their running shoes when they paid nocturnal visits to their computers.

During the day, while performing the pedestrian tasks for which she had been hired, Jilly worked in a small green room without windows. The air had a nothingness to it. It carried neither the salt of Nantucket nor the pollution of Boston. She captured enough fragments of Ingraham and his colleagues' work for the Wolpe Foundation to keep the philanthropic bureaucrats up to date about the experiments' progress and the money spent to achieve that. At the same time, she melded her obligatory duties to the professor with gathering information the Center. Much of the time, she understood little of what she was being asked to do. She worked late hours and heard from Beatrice Cruikshank that overwork was one of the prices one paid for working under a great man Jilly agreed.

CHAPTER 31

Interruption

"Is that Miss Carlson? You don't look like any Carlson I have ever known." A woman, hands on hips, stood in the doorway of Jillian's office. "You are my husband's friend, if I may call you that." A strange scent, not of the city, accompanied the woman and the twenty-something wearing a tweed coat, dirty shirt, and black riding boots who filled the remaining space of the doorway. Tanned, wrinkled, and thin lipped, the older woman gave the appearance of permanent anger and condescension.

Jilly had never seen either of them before, but the mention of the husband brought the quick realization that Philip's dragon wife had arrived. He had told Jilly that she never came to his office or to his lab. Their domestic spats had taken a slow diminuendo to an exhausted silence. Jilly rose in a confrontational stance and thought, *I could put the two of you on the floor quickly, but I will keep this verbal.*

"Who are you anyway? He usually takes on graduate students who can give him free research assistance in return for a letter of recommendation and some feeble love making. You don't look like a graduate student. Your clothes are better than most. Maybe an instructor's wife or girlfriend? I don't care. Maybe the odd tramp he picks up when he wants no conversation about germs and department politics?"

So this is Martha Hagedorn Ingraham, the outraged wife of my lover and companion in the arts. I suppose it was inevitable that we would meet. She's certainly right about Philip's fine calculations of women's vulnerabilities. He knows how far to go without risking refusal by his target and how far to go without forcing his wife into open warfare at a divorce court of her choosing. Martha did not leave. She stood silently in the door. So Jilly morphed from office worker into the asset Krushkin and his trainers meant her to be.

"I work on complicated computer problems for the professor and keep records of the research he and his associates perform. He wants to know about progress so that he can tell his grantors how things are going without needing to do more than push a button."

"Horse shit! You've been around longer than most, so I had the Pinckney Street apartment watched. You are practically living there. I know all about you. You supposedly live on Nantucket. By the way, where did you go to school? My detective can't find anything about you before you came to Massachusetts. Do you have relatives? Where are they? Who are they? Do you know what a fish fork is? Do you know how to use it? You claim to do high-level work, according to Philip. Horse shit! Where did you learn that?"

Jilly stood up and squared her shoulders. "According to my clients, I do satisfactory work. To me that is all that matters. I charge a fair price for what I know is good work. Where I studied or who my parents are is none of your business." Jilly liked being righteous; it was a seldom-used arrow in her quiver of duplicity.

The tight gray curls on Martha's head didn't budge as she moved forward under Jilly's nose. "If you think you can marry him, just remember this: the farm in Dover belongs to me. I inherited it, and you'll never get it. Philip has only what he earns here. The family money is mine to keep. I pulled him out of Kansas, put him through graduate school, and bribed editors to get his work published so that he can swindle foundations out of money to study germs. Not much integrity there. My attorneys have informed all the grand drug companies to have nothing to do with his so-called research, that it's all hocus pocus dreamed up by a farm boy from Kansas with ambitious parents. He is very smart, but not very clever about the practical side of life. You'll get tired of him when he's ten years older and you start to look for someone your own age. He doesn't put out the trash. He never learned to ride a horse."

Jilly had been trained to withstand the techniques that most countries' security services practiced. She had undergone difficult interrogations with the usual sleep and food deprivation caused by loud music and blows to the kidneys. On order, her classmates had buried her up to her neck and left her overnight just above the high water mark on a Black Sea beach while noise from the sea roared a meter from her ears.

Wifely indignation was altogether new. She kept silent and did not budge from her stance while the diatribe continued. "I am not a milksop." Everything in the office stayed silent and motionless, even the campus mail carrier remained by the door with her carriage of envelopes and boxes. No phone rang, and printers stopped clacking. Apparently this drama occurred whenever the professor had a friend who stayed more than a few nights at Pinckney Street. Martha finished quivering with rage while the female robot beside her kept eyes fixed on Jillian. After a few seconds of silence, Martha shoved aside the messenger's carriage and rushed through the door. Her wordless retainer followed. Listeners on the floor were delighted to have their morning infused with domestic drama.

One of the post docs stuck her head out. "Don't worry, Ms. Carlson. This happens all the time. Cameras at the doors and elevators will tell us when she came and when she left. That's good for the lawyers if she ever assaults you. She hit one of the professor's friends with a riding crop once." Finished with her reassurance, the woman closed her door like a turtle withdrawing into its shell. The office emitted a collective sigh, resumed its work, and wondered if Martha's threat, which seemed more strident and worried than the last time, would have any greater effect on Jillian that it had on Mary,

Joanna, or Isobel.

MARTHA'S WORDS were neither banal nor imperious nor wrong. She had, very simply, chosen the wrong man as her husband and, even worse, had elected to stay for the ride. The forces that had flung them together had not been thwarted by opposite pressures, nor did either wish that were so. They knew what they were doing. Each knew that the other had goals not normally associated with the marriage vows, and each believed that the other had gotten the lesser deal.

He tapped into her money and she into his prestige. The diminution of her wealth in a divorce was beyond her consideration. Besides, Martha Haledon Ingraham liked to receive invitations addressed to Professor and Mrs. Philip J. Ingraham, and her anger gave her a malignant joy. Martha would stay. Jillian feigned discomfort and embarrassment. She paused, brushed back her hair, and struck off for the lady's room.

That night he rolled his index finger from the nape of her neck to the crease of her buttocks. "Did she hurt you Jilly? I don't want that." She turned over and extended her arms. He was gentler than her captain, less mechanical, and certainly shyer.

MOST OF HER classmates had dreamed of finding a US spy in Moscow, filching the launch codes of the American missile system, forcing a submarine to the surface, or grabbing German economic plans that might not even be put into practice. Seducing a promising ballerina whose travels abroad would include her family was a less standard fantasy. Germ warfare lay on the radar scopes of very few.

Jilly's primary mission, she repeated to herself, remained to gather up all she could of Ingraham's work on the horror of mass infection while remaining undetected by foreign counterintelligence agencies and by her own colleagues. As for the professor, there was no talk, pillow or otherwise, about his work. When passion subsided, friendship might begin and offer its own dangers. Then their conversation might drift far enough to consider his ambitions and his work itself. That had not yet happened.

IN THE MEANTIME, she still worried about her encounter with 32. There may have been a few of her classmate stationed in Washington who traveled through Boston, but none on business. One senior Sluzhba fellow had traveled with his son to MIT to seek the boy's admission on the basis of his father's position in the Russian nomenklatura. The young admission's officer gave the son a long form he suggested be returned by December first. The father took this as a sign, as it would have been in Russia, that the application was a futile exercise. Had the boy's American guidance counselor not encouraged him to go ahead, the young man's candidacy would have died. But what had 32 been doing in town?

It was not a good sign. If he had seen her, how many others had? She had not looked him in the eye, which would have given them away to any watcher. *This operation*

CHAPTER 32

Charlie

JILLY KNEW she could afford few tears in the cloak that concealed her most critical work. Sometimes, though, the constant focusing wore her down. Charlie Banks provided an easy hiatus. They had become close friends after the inquest, nothing more, nothing less. Between the two, they knew most of the island's scabrous stories in their circle and exchanged them without hesitation. They had ritualized their singular conversations about the island whenever they attended the same gathering. Jilly would begin by admiring Charlie's well-gotten-up tweed suit, which he which wore from October to June. After living in America for months, Jilly knew the suit dated from almost another era. "Charlie when did you get that lovely suit? It looks very good on you." He would always answer that he could not recall the exact date, "but it was well after the Korean war."

"After I finished law school there wasn't much money left. I took a clerkship at Chatham and Hull, an old Boston firm. Partners wore jackets in the office and clerks had to remove their coats and hang them on pegs near the door. I had two suits then, one each for summer and winter. Nobody noticed what the clerks wore, and for three years I didn't buy another suit. When I left the firm, I decided that that I would stick to the one-suit policy however much money I made. In summer I wear the light gray version. It's cool, comfortable, no one seems to dislike it." Jilly leaned back as though contemplating Charlie's lecture on fashion acceptable on Nantucket Island. Other guests tended to leave them alone when it was clear from their whispers, which they punctuated with loud laughter, that they were exchanging the secrets of the temple.

This day, Charlie moved quietly and smoothly across the room and found Jilly sitting quietly by the fire. It took the dampness out of the air after a stretch of rain and fog. He had the valuable talent of being able to pass by or through a knot of talkers without being noticed. Jilly had seized a comfortable set of cushions and made room for him. The distance between them measured a friendship, not a romance.

A few out of earshot were curious; most were envious. Like the disappeared town crier of old, Charlie and Jilly were gossips. After ensuring that both knew the names of the Portuguese landscaper who had found his boss drunk and asleep under a bag of cuttings and helped him to bed, Jilly asked, "Charlie, transfer of properties and execution of wills must be very tedious. Anything exciting come across that lovely eighteenth-century Providence mahogany desk recently?" Jilly smiled and waited for a didactic answer.

"Jilly when I first practiced here I saved for six months in the hope that no one else would buy it. I got it before the tourists came?"

"Have you heard of Teddie's?"

"Of course. The bar that's a cover for gambling in the back room and hospitable ladies in the basement. Never been inside. I understand Teddie is a rich woman."

"She is. Stays below the radar. Last month she got exposed.

"Oh, fun. How?"

"She collects all the coins from the business, bags them, and sends them to a friendly bank in Providence. They are not declared. There, for a ten percent fee, a discrete banker turns them into paper money. Last month, her watchman fell asleep and three inebriated teenagers broke in, took the sacks, and piled them into a stolen car. They were so heavy that the rear end hit the road, destroyed the tail lights, and lost the bumper. A deputy pulled them over and arrested them for a double theft: car and coin. I was called in. The IRS man in Hyannis had availed himself of Teddie's services and agreed to look the other way. Likewise, the owner of the stolen car. The cases were dismissed. First time highjinks, a prank I offered the judge. I collected fees from Teddie, from the distraught parents, and from the car's owner, who had no license and spoke English poorly. All in all, a good morning's work. The total billings were fifty-two-hundred dollars, which you will see when you sum up the books. I try to protect my clients." Charlie and Jilly roared so loudly that a few turned to look at these usually quiet and sober members of their tight little circle.

CHAPTER 33

Manuelito

NOISE FROM MANUEL'S mower broke Jilly's thoughts. She looked out the window and saw him destroying the few blades of grass her front lawn had pushed up. There weren't enough clippings to rake. Jonah Coffin was right. No fertilizer in June, no grass in August. Manuel's son Manuelito loitered at the lawn's edge with a gas can, ready to refuel his father's ancient machine. The boy had no hat and looked hot standing there. "Manuelito come have a glass of tea." He glanced at his sullen father for approval and took small steps to Jilly's front door.

She knew from his father that Manuelito's visits violated an obscure code that lawn cutters and gardeners did not enter houses but restricted themselves to using toilets in the garage or used the woods. "Would you like sugar or milk? Or both?"

"Sugar, Senhora Jilly." Tea time happened about once a week, when Manuel conceived of a profit-making activity that was useful to Jilly. He was usually right, and his son came along every time. The boy's ancestors had come from Flores the westernmost island of the Azores, and the descendants of these Portuguese immigrants had been joined by later waves of those headed for the New World.

The Azorean community in Massachusetts and Rhode Island took hazardous jobs on fishing boats or menial jobs ashore. Some became shipowners, and George Enas bought land holdings that included the Nantucket Great Mill. When he died, a year after selling the mill, his widow, Sally, inherited everything. She left her estate to a trust that was established to help the deserving poor, especially the old.

Manuelito stood politely in Jilly's kitchen with that sad burden of history on his fragile shoulders. He knew little of his history, but he understood the ties of family and the hardships imposed by his father's inability to earn much cash. A neighbor cut his hair, his thrift-store tee-shirt celebrated the Woods Hole Oceanographic Center, and his jeans carried the odor of gasoline. He confessed with a shrug that he had not learned too much English as a small boy. His grandmother in New Bedford spoke only Portuguese, and she was the head of the family—not only there on the island, but in Fall River, New Bedford, and Fair Haven. After half-a-dozen visits Jilly concluded Nantucket was not an island but a cocoon of histories that only some of its denizens knew.

Manuelito is a virtual foreigner, but he drinks my tea like any good Russian who wandered into my house. Jilly liked the boy. He struck her as someone who would never steal the family's icons. She decided that she would begin his entrance into the island's society, and not at the back of a lawn mower. He was clearly smarter than 32 and better looking, too.

She sat him down and printed out the history of the Portuguese on Nantucket and Obed Macy's ancient story of the island's birth. Jilly picked out familiar words like "whaling." They discussed the mixed crews of Indians, English, and Manuelito's ancestors that took whales and how many of the crews jumped ship in Chile to escape cold and hunger when winter came. Then she showed him Chile on an antique globe in her living room. They discussed the failed voyages when captains and backers went broke. Jilly taught him that no matter the situation of your birth, your economic status could rise or fall. He liked that because he had taken a fancy to a pretty girl from a family that he and his own family believed lay beyond their reach.

One day, he said, "Senhora Jilly, the boys in school want to see you in a bikini at the beach." He knotted his fingers.

"Why, Manuelito?"

"Because they do not know who is prettier, you or Maria Fernandez."

"Who is Maria Fernandez?"

"She is a senior and very beautiful!"

"I'm sure she is very beautiful, but I seldom go to the beach."

"OK, Senhora. I just wanted to tell you the class is divided, half for you and half for Maria Fernandez."

"It is very thoughtful of you to tell me, but I am sure that Maria is prettier than I. Remember she is much younger."

"Ok, I will tell them."

CHAPTER 34

Settling in at the Lab

Jilly BECAME a familiar figure in the Biology Building as she came and went to Ingraham's office. Mrs. Cruikshank allowed that perhaps an outsider's extra set of eyes benefitted the professor's records and his reporting to the various entities that funded his projects. She kept hard copies of Jilly's reports and summations. She watched with satisfaction as the file grew larger and more incomprehensible. She confided to her circle of confidants that Miss Carlson attacked her computer rather than made use of it and that no evidence of intra-office hanky-panky had so far turned up.

Jilly HAD worked in the lab two days a week for a month, but by design had not entered Ingraham's office. She left each evening with the staff, took the subway to the Park Street Station, and went straight to Pinckney Street. She observed each day that none of the security arrangements had changed. This night, she told Ingraham that she would be late the next. One of his reports to Wolpe still puzzled her—she had trouble rearranging his scientific jargon into paragraphs that followed each other and could be read by the octogenarians of Wolpe's Board of Directors. Ingraham smiled. They washed the dishes together. They touched each other. She did not fall asleep. She wanted to feel the night. The soft rain began beating harder by the minute as it fell against the windows. Philip did not snore, but he breathed heavily. *These sheets are not as fine as the ones in Rothenburg,* Jilly mused, *but they are elegant and very soft and better than the ones at Yasenevo. And somehow very protective.*

In THE MORNING, Jilly hurried across Harvard Yard. She had begun to be recognized. A few not scurrying off to lectures stopped and chatted. She replied to honest questioners and gossip mongers alike that she worked for the professor only part time and that her other accounts kept her very busy. She allowed that her Nantucket business grew by leaps and bounds and that her time in Cambridge was brief and sure to become more so. Her listeners believed that Ingraham had acquired an uncommonly attractive and gifted mistress who would depart for greener pastures once the faux adolescent passions had subsided. She was not a PhD candidate, had no degree as far as anyone knew, and probably wouldn't last a semester. These mild tales added themselves to Ingraham's biography, almost a spoof by then, and to the store of the university's anecdotal history, *but not much more*, they thought.

She said hello to Mrs. Cruikshank and the postdocs. (Whether Mrs. Cruikshank had received good value for her reportage on Philip and Jilly was not apparent. Her conversation on the subject only confirmed to the uninformed what mostly all had earlier accepted as a new, but not unexpected truth.) The former growled a return, the latter said Hi. Jilly slipped into her memories. Even the Marxist atheists had greeted her at the door with: "May God give you a good day."

She shuffled into her tiny office, grander than her previous corner in the lab, but smaller than her space in Petersburg, took her laptop out of her backpack, and began working. She left a stack of jottings, dairies, cancelled checks, and lab reports on her desk. In Saint Petersburg, that kind of work would have been left to the clerks. Here it was better to suggest to passersby that much remained to do before she cleared up Professor Ingraham's chaotic record system. A few self-interested colleagues commented that it was just in time, grants could be lost because of erroneous filings.

THE NEXT NIGHT, Jilly stayed late as she had told Philip she would. To the office staff, she cited the pile of paper on her desk, mostly with Wolpe headings. Jilly waited until the guard passed, set her timer for seventeen minutes, and picked the lock. She knew where she had left off and started transcribing formulas that mystified her. The copied files were written as though scribbled by an informed but probably chaotic mind. Either that or they had been encrypted on a very sophisticated system that might take weeks to break.

Jilly knew straightaway that only a biologist of Ingraham's stature would understand the jumble of symbols, words, and figures that Jilly had filched. Jilly's algorithms in Saint Petersburg bore no resemblance to what flashed across the monitor. The timer on Jilly's watch showed two minutes left before she had to get back to her desk. Once there, she punched the computer's keys for a few moments in case the guard came on schedule and peered inside the office. He did, looked around, said good evening, and left. Jilly waited a decent interval and returned Ingraham's computer to its normal protected status. She put on her coat and took a taxi to Pinckney Street with the thumb drive in her laptop bag. Philip opened the door before she knocked. She mixed every fruit in the kitchen and put them in Ingraham's blender. She drained the container. They had no supper and little talk. Their passion increased. Friendship and solicitude crept into the room and did not disturb them.

She left Pinckney Street in the morning, worked at the lab, and bused to the Hyannis Ferry. Ingraham had social duties with his wife in Dover and Prides Crossing that he could not avoid without energizing his wife's smoldering fury at this most attractive of all her husband's mistresses.

JILLY'S SOCIAL LIFE on the island continued happily. She accepted one invitation that weekend to a banker's party. Dull she knew, but desirable for cover and good relationships with the rich islanders. A Mrs. Stolipin risked what others had would not and asked Jilly about her background and her love for Nantucket. The inquisitor somehow mentioned snakes, which she alleged to loathe. Jilly recounted the growth on the island of that slithery population years ago and how the islanders, not knowing which were poisonous and which not, dug holes into which all snakes of whatever denomination were raked. Fires were started above the holes and the snakes died either from suffocation or from overcooking. Mrs. Stolipin blanched at this gory but truthful bit of the island's early history and stepped back. She forced a smile and, defeated, went in search of her husband who, she promised, would refill her drink. Jilly drove home alone.

Sunday passed, a 10K run, and an examination of which plants, shrubs and flowers had failed her. A meditation on the mission's progress, tradecraft, Sluzhba regulations, and her security measures and emergency signals demanded several hours. She sought balance in her professional and private life and did not find it. After dinner she took to her bicycle and went to the site of her cache. She retook bearings and ensured that the markers had not changed. She noted that several trees were taller and that the walk into the wood appeared untouched by human activity. Horan could arrest her on the spot if he found Jilly's treasure. She put on her red safety jacket and rode home as the moon appeared. She thought for a few moments of oysters and beer. She slept well that cool night.

CHAPTER 35

Blue Jeans

THE PUTT-PUTT of Manuelito's mower disturbed Jilly's wake-up routine. Manuel began at nine, his son at 7:30. Jilly signaled hello through the window and made coffee. She dressed and sat at her desktop computer working through the income and outflow of the Czech lady's gift shop. She had enough gift wrapping for the next three Christmases and had failed to anticipate strong sales of her most profitable dolls. She had to Fedex emergency shipments at extravagant cost. Jilly had proven what she had initially perceived—the owner ran the shop for herself, not to profit.

A knock on the kitchen door slowed Jilly's descent into sympathetic rage over her client's fecklessness. "Manuelito, have you finished already?"

"Yes, Senhora Jilly, and the weeds are gone too."

"Brilliant, Manuelito, would you like iced tea? I made it up yesterday night and chilled it overnight for you." Jilly handed him the glass. A smell emanated from Manuelito that brought her back to a tank exercise when she had been ordered to serve as assistant gunner. The closed tank reeked of diesel oil, cordite, and body odor. "Manuelito, did you spill that mix of gas and oil on yourself?"

"Yes, Senhora." She had watched as his father deposited at the bottom of the driveway a five-gallon can of fuel the boy could barely lift, let alone pour.

"Manuelito maybe those pants can't be cleaned." Jilly knew that the father would probably deliver two hard slaps across his son's face. "I think we had better get you another pair. I will pay for them since the accident happened while you helped me."

"How can we do that?"

"Stand right there, do not sit down. I will get a measuring tape." Jilly fetched a cloth measuring tape from her hutch's drawer and measured Manuelito's leg and waist. No woman except his mother and the school doctor had ever touched him, and he had strange feelings. "Thirty-inch waist and thirty-inch leg, Manuelito. Easy to remember. Tell your parents that you tripped over something I had left in your way in the garage or that I slipped and spilled gasoline that you cleaned up for me. Tell them I said you did a good job today, especially on the weeds that I had neglected. Next time, take the edging tool and cut along the border of the flowers."

"Thanks, Senhora Jilly. I will tell my father it was an accident and I should not be blamed." The boy put his empty glass on the counter and left. The smell of gas and oil remained. Jilly placed an order with Bean for two pairs of light blue jeans, 30x30, and two medium t-shirts.

CHAPTER 36

Oeillade

THE MEAL was finished, and it was good. "Philip, do many Harvard professors cook and wash dishes and keep a cellar of wines?"

"Hardly Jilly, but they all live well." There are a few geniuses out there, but most simply profess for very good salaries. One man across the river gets a small fortune for teaching and a second, larger one, for babbling to people who like to hear him because he tells them that they are brilliant cutting-edge business men. I've heard him, he babbles. Another fellow gives the same lecture on the French Revolution that he gave when I was an undergraduate. He was a PhD candidate then and is about to retire now. He's certainly made a good living out of the guillotine. Another fellow reads *Beowulf*, stays drunk all summer at Marblehead, and comes back every fall dead sober to teach the same old *Beowulf*. I look for something new, and every three or four months, I pierce my ignorance. It's a thrill beyond understanding to see a something that nobody else has ever discovered."

"An old fellow who wears a yellow scarf, wrapped around his neck knows my name. He has large teeth, also yellow, and always says, "Good evening, Miss Carlson. Off to Old Fizzy are we? Who is he and how does he know my name?"

"Oh, don't worry, Jilly. That's Oldsworthy. He knows every name in the Yard, been teaching medieval Portuguese literature since the flood. Same lectures. He uses "Old Fizzy" because that was the nickname of the old Astro-Physics building that was torn down to be replaced by the very useful structure in which you proudly work. Say 'fine,' and he'll go away."

He's harmless except to the few students who sit in front of him. He works in a dead world where everything and everybody have been exhumed, examined, and explicated. His scholarship faces no risk. My post docs and I are fairly sure of what our work will turn out tomorrow, but we know that by next year some of our calculations will have been shown to be wrong, many of our experiments will fail, and we will start over. And of course some of our findings will disprove our theories. Often a necessary step."

"Does the Wolpe Foundation understand the value of negative findings?"

"We face risk, the snickers of our colleagues, and dried-up grants, yes. When we work we want to have good failures. They teach us we're approaching success.

Oldsworthy, on the other hand, lives in a tranquil world of capital letters and semicolons.

"Ever think of going back to school and joining us, Jilly? Though not, I presume, as a biologist."

"Maybe. Am I some new thing that you will finish off in an article before you hurry on to your next discovery?"

"Jilly, you are cruel."

"Philip, I'm not the first to occupy that lovely bed in the next room. Did you cook for them too?" Pans clanged, faucets ran, and the dishwasher rumbled.

"The best thing about history, Jilly, is that it's gone, never to be seen or heard again. A few who of those who hate me most around here view my social life with envy. Others with admiration. They're wrong. Lust abounded. Pleasure was given and taken. Affection? Some. Care? No. These triumphs signaled failure of the worst sort. Martha Hagedorn is the worst hurt of all. I don't know where you fit, but you have made me happy and confused. Now I worry only that one of my colleagues will find a mistake in my lab work and publish it to the world."

"That's very flattering confession, Philip."

JILLY'S DAYS began to acquire a sameness. She did not visit Mayfield for a month. There were no emergency signals; no cantankerous sermons clouded her day. She would have to walk up the stairs to his sad office before she next left for the island, though. The stays at Pinckney Street had shorter meals and longer nights. "Jilly," Philip asked when they lay on the bed, ready to sleep, "do you know what *oeillade* means? I give you several every time we meet."

"No, dear Philip, I do not."

"It means an amorous glance."

"Turn off the light, Philip."

THE NEXT DAY, Jilly's worked regular hours at Ingraham's office. She slipped out at noontime and headed to Mayfield's office. The two-way trip interfered with her workday but she had to go. Mayfield met her at the door. They exchanged signals that indicated silence. Mayfield put on a shabby raincoat. They walked outside. "Jilly the Center reported back that you are on the right track. The last drive had some new material that we lacked but were about to produce on our own. Your take saved time. The formulas are sent in code; the Wolpe crowd has hired an expensive security firm to protect Ingraham's work. I am to tell you not to worry about the research itself, but to concentrate on any work you believe to be connected to the fuse. Why are you so professional and respectful to me, Jilly wondered as she injested Mayfield's brief. He's a shit at heart. Maybe he sees a dacha for himself. They parted like coworkers after a lunch that satisfied. Jilly always carried a sewing kit with a ricin needle in the tiny second slot. She could never walk down Dartmouth Street without musing about that needle's potential.

She returned to the office and then left several hours later with the evening crowd to the Harvard Square subway. Walking to the station, she felt a boosted confidence in her ability to complete the mission. The target environment had not changed at work—no cameras inside, roving guard every twenty minutes, his door locked, and piles of paper on Mrs. Cruikshank's desk. Motion detectors were not appropriate there, and she failed to find any listening devices. The lab itself would have the best place to install them, if only to catch results of the post docs' successes as they performed their silent work from eight to five. Their successes did not arrive in bottles of clear fluid or CAT scans but in lines of formal reporting on progress and the expenditures it had required. Jilly knew little more about their lives and research now than when she had begun her work for Ingraham.

CHAPTER 37

The Young Boy and the Land

ON NANTUCKET, Jilly worked in the spare bedroom on the mounds of clutter she brought back from her accounts in Boston. The work was petty, almost insultingly so. How could a shop owner bill for five-dozen two-foot Chinese dolls and write in three dozen to stock? Yasenevo and English House had prepared her for hardship and mortal situations, but not boredom. If capitalism suffocated its minions, why did so many want it? Every two hours, Jilly went outside and did stretching exercises. It seemed that Jonah Coffin walked, plucked weeds, or tested the weather every morning that Jilly worked at home. They waved at each other like long-lost friends.

MANUELITO WALKED up the driveway at noon. He wore half of what Jilly had bought him, one yellow T-shirt and a pair of light blue jeans. He smiled. "You look wonderful Manuelito! Do they fit?"

"Yes, Senhora Jilly, they fit perfect. My mother and my father thank you very much. My father telephoned my grandmother in New Bedford and told her what you did. She said thank you in Portuguese. She doesn't speak English,"

"How long has your family lived here?"

"Couple of hundred years. We come from the island nearest here, Flores. It is tiny, full of fishermen. Grandmother still votes for the Portuguese City Councilors and pays taxes only if the Commissioner is Portuguese."

"What if she doesn't pay?"

"It is all arranged. Grandmother is very loyal."

"Manuelito, you and your family are fine people."

"Here I brought you books" The boy produced a dog eared copies of *Catcher in the Rye* and *The Old Man and The Sea*.

"I haven't read these in a long while. Have you tried them? The *Old Man* book says that a boy becomes a man when he buys an older man a beer. Do you believe that?"

"No!"

"Good. Don't buy beer for anyone, especially yourself. How did a tuna kill your uncle?"

"No, Senhora, after my uncle was killed by a tuna off Provincetown, my grandmother told her sons that two-hundred years of fishing was enough. Before you came, the men leaned over the side of the trawler and gaffed tuna who struggled in the net. The men waited until the waves lifted the nets and gaffed the tuna and waited until the next rise and they used the next wave to pitch the tuna over their left shoulder. If the man did not pull hard enough the tuna's tail would hit you. Sometimes it hit hard. My uncle slipped as his tuna came up. The tuna hit him in the neck and broke it. He died right away. We were all sad, but we knew it would happen. My uncle was not as strong as the other men. Josito was a baby and they had to eat and rent a house. Auntie Esmerelda had to work. Work on the land, save money, and buy a house. She has a nice house That's what I am doing, working hard to buy a house one day.

Jilly changed the subject. ""Manuelito I think nothing in those books can teach you very much. But read them anyway."

"Good. Let's get back to work! Don't buy beer for anyone, especially yourself. "Thank you, Senhora. We all like you. Even the tourist man from Boston says you are very nice. He saw you around your flower garden."

"Thank you, Manuelito. Who is this man."

"He says you are very smart, and he wanted to know what you do here. I told him you had a nice house."

"He saw me?"

"Yes, Senhora, when you were exercising outside."

"What else did he say?"

"Nothing except that you were very interesting."

"If he asks you again say nothing about me! What did he look like?"

"Almost like one of us. He wore sun glasses and a dark summer jacket."

"Thanks. Now go water every inch that you think is dry. And no gas or oil on your new clothes. After you finish, come have a glass of cold tea."

CHAPTER 38

Followed

JILLY HAD OBEYED Krushkin's First Law. Act on instinct. Don't waste time thinking. By the time you reach a conclusion, it will be too late, you will be in trouble. She had sensed while walking across the Common that she was being trailed. She concluded that it was not 32 from Philadelphia. He was too frightened. Nor was it Horan. He knew where she was and who Mayfield was and what Jerry did for her. If Horan were on the scent, Jilly knew precisely what steps he would take. For him it would be a long and rocky trail. To trail her every step would have required teams of agents at Logan, the ferry dock, the fishing dock, the bus stations in Hyannis, and at Park Square. That was too expensive for a subject who had given no hard evidence of being up to mischief. This man conducted an amateur surveillance, he was clumsy and asked the wrong person the wrong questions. Martha Hagedorn knew about Jilly and needed no further information. So she was out, too. So it was likely a blunderer who would foul everyone's nest.

If Jilly told Mayfield, he would bluster that the operation had been compromised, that the fault was hers, and that she had better be brought home before she did further damage. Better to do nothing she concluded. If the fellow in the dark summer jacket showed his face again, she would know he had not been replaced, as a professional team would have arranged, but had acted on his own or would sell Jilly to a competitive intelligence organization once he had tangible evidence of her perfidy. She smelled incompetence and a lack of professional knowledge.

THE NEXT TIME she went to the city, she ferried and bused. From Park Street Station she took the subway to Lechmere, waited on the platform, and returned to Park Street. The Lechmere platform had been empty for fifteen minutes, and no one ran up the stairs to board Jilly's train at the last minute. She walked to Dartmouth Street along the side of the Common. There were flowers on only one side as she walked down Newbury Street. Sad, she wanted to look at all the flowers on earth and smell each one. She climbed the stairs to Mayfield's quietly and hated the brown-yellow walls that surrounded her. She knocked softly and entered. She spoke of an old account that had gone bad and handed Mayfield the thumb drive. She wrote: Security?

He wrote: *Nothing changed or new. No communications from the Center.* She held up five fingers. He opened his old iron safe and counted out five-thousand dollars.

Bastard, he wouldn't tell me if the whole FBI was waiting outside to arrest me. She pointed to the used drive and signaled for a new one like a trader buying bonds in Chicago. He took one from a right-hand drawer and handed it to her, all the while commiserating about the bad account.

"Bad luck, Jilly, maybe they'll pay if their fall school lines sell. At least it's a tax deduction."

"Please no more of these, Jerry."

CHAPTER 39

Josito

THE NEXT MORNING, Jilly awoke as from a nightmare. Smells and motion came from the other side of her bed. She had no gun or knife. She made a fist, knuckles out, of her right hand and pointed the fingers on her left. She turned quickly, expecting an attack. She turned and found a five-year-old boy dressed in shabby clothes curled up on the next pillow and fully asleep. The putt-putt of Manuelito's mower interrupted. She wrapped a sheet around herself and went to the kitchen window. "Manuelito," she shouted, "who is that boy in my bed? What is he doing here?"

"Senhora Jilly, that is my cousin Josito. He is ashamed he tripped over out other uncle's oil can this morning and left the garage. He could not go home because his father is dead and his mother, Auntie Esmerelda, works in a hotel."

"Why did he come here?"

"Because he knows where I am."

"And why did he go to sleep in my bed?"

"We all like you, Senhora Jilly, and Josito always goes to sleep when he is alone. I told him to follow me this morning and he would be safe. He is too young to work on the boats, and he has no mower."

"He smells awful, Manuelito."

"He played football yesterday, and his other clothes weren't dry. He likes the smell of your bed."

"Doesn't he have spare clothes?"

"No, Senhora, only two jeans. They are poor."

"Has he had breakfast?"

"Probably not. His mother leaves early."

"Tell him that I am not angry and to go outside while I dress. Then we will have breakfast."

"OK, Senhora Jilly. He does not speak English yet. He will start school next year, but he may not go, he is ashamed because the family is poor and doesn't have the right clothes or a T-shirt for football."

Jilly boiled eggs and cooked slices of bacon. She had no sweet rolls, only dark bread with butter and jam. She made tea, and the three ate in silence. Jilly rose and took out her cloth tape measure. "Manuelito, tell Josito I will measure his waist and his leg."

"Ok, Senhora. Josito, em pe." The lad stood stock still while Jilly performed this unusual task. She took a beach robe from her closet.

"Manuelito, you can go back to mowing. Please tell Josito to take off his clothes in the laundry room and put them in the washing machine. He can wear this robe and sleep on the couch until the clothes are done. Tell him to put his sneakers in, too, they are filthy. Can he use a washing machine and a dryer, Manuelito?"

"I tried to teach him, but he is too short and cannot pour the soap very well."

"Then you set the washer going. I must work now. Keep track of him." She measured the boy again. He was too thin, something was wrong.

"Thank you, Senhora Jilly. We all like you." Jilly gave her instructions with a firmness just short of her instructors' directions on an exercise at Yasenevo in winter mud.

The business of giving orders and the expectation that they would be followed came back easily. It took a moment for her to return to her role as the owner of a small business, the mistress of a prominent scientist, an admired member of Nantucket society, and an agent of the Russian Intelligence service. Jilly returned to her office in the second bedroom and worked until noon. There had been no sound from the living room, and Jilly saw the boy still asleep with a piece of black bread clutched in his right hand.

The boys left after lunch in clean clothes and better nourished, and Jilly returned to her state of savored solitude. The phone rang at 1:30. "Yes, Bob how are you?" *Another visit with Lothar and his hair growing down to his eyes?* "I'm busy all the rest of the week. Late this afternoon is free. See you then." Horan served up his words as more an obligation than as a favor. No mention that: "You can bring your lawyer, but it won't be necessary."

CHAPTER 40

Tested

The Washington counterintelligence crowd must think they have something or maybe they are simply filling out forms and checking off the boxes. On the other hand, I wasn't declared a person of interest, and he didn't say it was in my best interest to have a lawyer present at the interview. No one followed me to the cache site, and nobody followed me back. Nobody saw my thumb drives.

Jilly pedaled down to Horan's office at 4:30. "Jilly, this is Jack McGill, an old friend who comes here, he claims, to work but really to swim, eat lobster, and drink beer. Jack, this is Jillian Carlson, our resident computer expert."

"Nonsense, Bob, I'm just an amateur who keeps books and records that other people here can't or don't want to"

They all smiled. McGill had an office worker's white skin and a barely sincere handshake. He picked his fingernails. He mouthed a just audible: "Glad to meet you, Jillian." The three exchanged trite pleasantries. McGill's query about where to find the best 'real lobster' touched a low point in banality. The cadence and the accent of his few words told Jilly that he had been brought up in a bilingual family or that English was not his first language.

They entered the conference room and sat down at the long brown table overseen by an air conditioner high on the wall. A picture of a trio of geese in flight hung over Jilly's head. Jack sat and waited for Horan to speak. He was subordinate to the purpose of the meeting and seemed not to want to be in Nantucket in Horan's office with Jillian Augusta Carlson.

He was pudgy and wore a colorless tie that matched nothing in his other clothes. His cheeks drooped with a permanence that no swim or other exercise could rectify. His shoes were not scuffed, but old and cracked. He grasped his files with small weak hands, and Jilly concluded that far from wanting to swim, he had no athletic skills or desires. He was not a person who would want to swim among the island's tricky currents and tidal flows. Despite the air conditioning, he perspired.

Horan began: "Jilly, we have extended our research into the computer hacking that we discussed before. We are a bit closer to a solution. I am going to show you some pictures. Some of the people in them may be involved in our research, maybe none. That's where you come in. You lived in Europe and worked there, as I understand."

Jillian broke the flow of Horan's questioning. The pudgy little visitor stood and falsely adjusted his shirt. He said little. Jillian asked him, "Do you work in computers?"

"No, only a little at the office."

"Here are twenty photos, Jilly. Could you look at them and tell us if you have ever seen any of the faces?"

She looked thoughtfully at the images and kept her reactions under control. Among the twenty were Willy, the hotel owner in Copenhagen, and the dentist who filled the cavity before Jilly left Denmark. Jilly identified Willy. "This one, Bob. I worked for him. He owned the hotel where I stayed in Copenhagen. He's rough around the edges, but a decent fellow. *Good old Willy.* He was very good to me. That job was where I learned all about EU regulations. I did every office job for him: kept records, filed financial reports for Germany and the EU, and paid his taxes and license fees. It's where I got the practical education I use in my business."

" "Good, Jilly. Anyone else?"

"Bob, I remember this face, the bland fellow, he's from Copenhagen. But he has a very Danish face, so I'm not sure how well I am distinguishing him from a couple of others."

"I am going to shuffle these photos. Look at them again. Whom do you remember?" Jilly scanned the photos and again picked out Willy and the man who was almost certainly her dentist.

"That's it, Bob. One for sure and one possible." Jack sat and watched Jilly speak. He said nothing. Jilly knew from her hours in the language lab that this unattractive little man watched her lips as she spoke. *He's trying to gauge if English is my native language, if I am compensating for short vowels, and if any Slavic gutturals come through. He probably isn't a linguist, only a consultant from the horde of underemployed Middle-Europeans on the East Coast. Creepy bastards! I hope his talent is as shabby as his clothes.*

Jack and Horan nodded to each other. "Bob, I'll be in Boston, Somerville, and Cambridge the next three days. Leave voice mail if you need anything." Horan nodded.

"Thanks, Jilly, you don't know how much help you've given me." McGill nodded goodbye. Jilly found her bicycle and pedaled home. Much help meant that he either eliminated Jilly or put her on a watch list.

It was warmer than it had been. Jilly remembered a lecture given at the Hermitage on an Albrecht Durer sketch. A group of monkeys danced happily until someone threw a nut into the middle of their dance. Their actions and mood changed as each tried to get the nut. *Who is the monkey, and who is the nut? I know I was a happy monkey an hour ago. I think that I have just become the nut.*

She went over her emergency procedures. Horan and maybe Lothar would await a phone call or text message to her contact warning them that Willy and the dentist had been made. She checked the bedroom. Better this time, Bob, but not perfect. The layer of dust on her dining table had blown away, probably when they opened the door. A strong off shore breeze blew over the island that afternoon. She had conquered her opponents' tired gimmickry. Maybe, she thought, they had returned to wherever and checked off the search box. Jilly slept well. Searches and interrogations were as much part of her life as completing the mission. Still, Horan was getting close to the bone.

CHAPTER 41

Download

JILLY FLEW TO LOGAN on the first flight and bused to Boston. She took the subway and walked half a mile to her appointment. No three-man surveillance. She sped up, entered a store with a pay phone, and dialed her emergency number. A female voice answered. Jilly said 62. The six identified Copenhagen, and the two indicated the number of contacts either uncovered or suspected of servicing the Sluzhba. That operation would be shut down immediately. She prayed that Lars and Helga would escape whatever net the German service put out.

Lars followed orders from Jacobsson and knew little, but Helga's career as a full-time mother was about to begin if an enterprising operator from the Danes tracked her movements. She would not weep, she had seen and done too much to be sentimental about bumps in the road. Helga liked meeting new people and eating good meals at the Sluzhba's expense. If she broke under the BND's interrogation, she would identify Jilly by name. If the Sluzhba pulled her out, her children would lack the mothering and western education Helga craved for them. If Helga stayed and were constantly tracked, she forever risked trial and imprisonment. German law and punishment for espionage lacked the severity of the Cold War years, but still involved jail time—more as an example to others than as retribution for crimes that did not involve blood. But Helga . . .

JILLY DELIVERED her accounting work to the manager of a three-store chain of merchandise that, she concluded from the inventory she tracked, contained nothing a civilized buyer would ever want. He always paid his bill to Mayfield on time and in full. She used waterproof lipstick, not her shade, to write 62 on the back of an agreed upon bench on the Common. When Jilly made no contact with Mayfield, he would look there for a signal.

Her pursuers, if any, didn't know her plans for the day. It had enough normal twists and turns to eliminate any conclusion that Jilly intended to elude pursuit. She climbed up the stairs from the Park Street subway and headed toward Faneuil Square. She had studied the old Boston and didn't like the massive new buildings that had ruined an interesting skyline. She phoned her next appointment, a large family-owned pharmacy that had survived the chain drugstores' invasion. The store was sufficiently large that it had a list of voicemail options. She told a voice she would arrive later than they had planned. The voice replied that it was fine, and hung up. She stopped at a shop, looked at eyeglass frames, and told the clerk who swooped down on her that she spent too much time on her computer and would soon need prescription lenses. He smiled. Jilly left the store calculating the risk of visiting an eye doctor who kept records about customers and the cost of lenses and frames.

The day's business done, Jilly went to the lab, said hello to the guards and Mrs. Cruikshank, and unloaded her laptop onto her desk. The postdocs labored with their glass and metal apparatus, and the minutes ticked by. Ingraham was not there, and his door was closed. Jilly pulled scribbled notes from a pile marked Wolpe. Diminishing that ever-refilled pile of paper justified her presence. She was tempted to write her summaries in Russian with the notion that no one but she would ever read them and that they would, in any case, be as intelligible for the drowsy Wolpe readers in Russian as in English.

The office emptied. Only the occasional scuffle of the postdocs broke the silence. Funny how they made more noise at the end of the day. When their Nikes reached a muffled crescendo, she knew they were about to leave, always together. *Were they scared that one would steal a march on the other by staying late instead of riding the subway or bus to God knows where?* Philip entertained a condescending attitude toward his probably loyal help. One night he told Jilly that the taller one wanted babies to assure her role as an agent of humanity's inevitability. The other wanted babies only after she had married a gentleman, preferably a well-landed gentleman from the Midwest. She would return to the lab after a decent interval. That was all he ever said about them.

JILLIAN WAITED until silence had settled. The guard that night was new to her; he followed a different schedule. He passed the office every eighteen minutes and opened the door to scan the outer office and listen. Mayfield had congratulated Jilly for her last download. Apparently she had invaded Ingraham's possibly final conclusions about how germs could be transported and stored. Ingraham lacked the final element of his work. No one had ever executed the results of his endeavors. She fumbled as she inserted the thumb drive, broke a string of passwords and began downloading where she had left off. She downloaded formulas and short sets of directions written in a language probably known only to a few dozen people scattered over the world and suddenly came to the end.

A note stated that one particular avenue research of several years had ended. He warned that a one-size fuse bought off the shelf would not fit his bomb package, and he included formulas that would lead the metal turners to the correct piece of gear after they had completed a few experiments. The task was best left to the metal benders because the fuse would need portability, which demanded the use of certain metals with which he was not adequately familiar. *We are far ahead of the competition and some tasks would best be left to the electronics crowd. Thanks are extended to the Wolpe Foundation, its Board of Directors, and Harvard University for their help in completing this very important work.* That the final phase of the research had not been encrypted astounded Jilly. To send the fruits of years of work openly surprised and confused. She read more and came upon a lengthy file encrypted with an ultra-sophisticated system. Ingraham had sent on that copy to his funders and stored one copy for himself, presumably one he could edit at leisure.

JILLY CAME LATE that night to Pinckney Street. She and Philip had decided without words that they would have short suppers and, occasionally, a celebratory feast with lobster or fine meat and wine from his cache. Jilly showered more to shed the day's evils than to remove the grime and sweat of a hurried city existence. They were both tired. When he was in her she felt the same ecstasy as their first night but also an added feeling that she could identify only as solace. Nobody had given her that before. Next morning, they parted silently with the understanding that the day would be lacking without the other's presence.

CHAPTER 42

Precautions

THE FERRY TIED up with an aunt's kiss. So gentle was the landing that the passengers hesitated before pushing toward the gangway. Jilly got off and headed toward the laundry room at The Cottages, where she had permission to deposit her locked bicycle. She kept records for the beautiful black girl who ran the resort. The ride home did not hold its usual tang. She heard the lawn mower before she saw it and remembered that Manuelito had cut the grass the previous week. "How are you, Senhora Jilly?"

"Fine, Manuelito. How are you and Josito?"

"Oh, we are fine. He came with me this morning, helped to fill the mower with gas, and now he is asleep on the sofa."

"It's good that he helps you, but how did he get into the house when the doors are both locked?"

"It was arranged, Senhora Jilly. He likes you very much." Jilly passed the sleeping boy, went to her office, and closed the door. *My God, am I running an orphanage, a day-care Center, a soup and lobster kitchen, or a child-smuggling ring? What would Horan think if he stumbled into Josito taking his morning nap?*

Jilly spent the morning balancing inventory against sales and damaged goods for a chain of hardware stores. *Why,* she argued to herself, *must I do the accountants' work for them?* She ran ten kilometers and made lunch for three. "Josito says he wants to learn English so that he can talk with you, Senhora Jilly."

"I hope he will, Manuelito."

"Josito says the short man in the dark coat is glad that we are helping you because you are very nice and very smart."

"You saw him again? Where?"

"At the football field where Josito watches because he is not old enough and does not have soccer shoes like mine."

"Did he ask you where I was or what I was doing?"

"He asked us when you come back. I told him I did not know."

"Manualito, tell me if he comes again and what he asks." The lunch ended in polite silence. "Josito and I thank you. We have told Grandmother in New Bedford that you are nice, and she says thank you."

JILLY FACED THE UNEXPECTED. She could not telephone Mayfield soon after leaving Boston. His phone is probably tapped anyway. She could not call her emergency number for exfiltration orders. That would be to admit her failure to complete the mission.

Jilly worked at home for a week. She avoided communication with Mayfield. She put a few of Ingraham's memos and records in better order but worked mostly for Sconset Bank and the hospital. Their tasks held moderate interest for her, and they paid on time.

SHE TOOK THE FERRY to Hyannis and the nonstop bus to Boston. She telephoned her appointment and told the accounting manager that she would come after lunch. He was lazy, disorganized, and mildly rude. Jilly did most of his work for him and overcharged the firm. She walked down Newbury Street, stopping at stores in the hope of finding an outfit that would lift her appearance from working girl into something Philip might prefer. She had gotten the notion that Philip did not appreciate her wearing pants suits. He had not illogically offered suggestions for replacements.

She was not watching for a trailer, and any alert watcher would take her for what she was at that moment, an ardent explorer for clothes that would raise her a notch on Nantucket and perhaps in the eyes of Professor Philip Ingraham. Despite the glitz of the beautiful displays, she slipped into thoughts of dignified successful Russians struggling for the necessities and the few luxuries on sale in Saint Petersburg. The memories stung, and they dimmed her excitement for a moment.

MAYFIELD WENT unvisited for weeks. Words to him were useless. She sent a thumb drive to another address in the full knowledge that she neared the end of the formulas, directions, and commentary that she could glean from Ingraham and the postdocs' computers.

In the meantime, she had become more than fond of the new men in her life. Josito would need soccer shoes and a coat in order to attend school. Manuelito would opt for heavy jeans. She had ascended from hiring them to conceiving an interest in them, to feeding them, to addressing some of their extended family's problems. Her relationship with them had built a life of its own separate from her business cover, her life as Krushkin's minion, and her enthronement as Philip's mistress. Her father's life had an authenticity and genuineness about it. She thought, "I'm living a bad novel." Hers seemed burst from a two-ruble adolescents' novel.

SHE SPENT MORE TIME thinking about what Philip wanted and how she might handle him when her mission was accomplished than she thought prudent. Ingraham did not serve as an agent and showed no signs of wanting to alter his career path by working for a foreign government. He produced his wares and, after all was said and done, was the owner of data coveted by many. The Wolpe Foundation and their providers had divined that need and written up requirements that could be broadly interpreted. Essentially, they let Ingraham pursue his own lines, bricolage the French called it, tinker and put themselves first in line to acquire a distinguished researcher for his project. The transfer to the Center of those data were the sole purposes of Jilly's residence in Massachusetts. Wolpe got its rewards, the Center received its crown jewel.

JILLY TELEPHONED Mayfield to complain that his monthly check was late and that a family business in Malden had not called her to complete a five-year history of their transactions. They had mixed family money with the income and expenses of their business. The IRS had demanded that the business's books be separated from the family's.

Mayfield replied with an oily smugness that Jilly's check lay on his desk and she was more than welcome to pick it up. That meant that the last thumb drive had been received by the Center; it contained Ingraham's conclusions about remote detonations of different families of biological agents. Mayfield offered no rebuke to Jilly for the encryption of the data. She knew that given time, her colleagues could break any proprietary code. Mayfield's tone indicated that he could now get rid of Jilly, payments to her, her use of him as a mail box, and the secure administration needed to assist an aggressive black operative. Jilly's repeated refusal to engage in sex humiliated him, and she guessed that he had already asked the Center for her removal to Moscow or her assignment to another mission distant from Nantucket and Boston.

JILLY CHECKED the hand rail for the scratch that warned her not to continue up the stairs and to leave at once. It was pristine. Jilly pushed open the unlocked door, entered, and gazed for the last time, she hoped, at the dirty brown walls. They exchanged all clear signals and removed the SIM cards from their phones. "Jilly the news is very, very good. That troublesome account called and explained the misunderstanding. You can return there and finish your work. Only a day or two more before we can close the account, get a check from them to me, and then I pay you. It's been a wait, but everything is in order."

That sounds like a dismissal from the head instructor at Yasenevo. Had he asked for a replacement already? No Jerry, I am not leaving, she promised herself. She flashed the fingers on both hands, indicating ten-thousand dollars. Mayfield went to his old iron safe and pulled out a package of mixed bills. Jilly had enough run-away money in her cache on Nantucket, but her ever-increasing entertainments and antique purchases consumed more than she made at both her legitimate jobs. Wolpe paid well, but not that well. She had to buy Philip an occasional case of Moselle. It did not surprise her that Jed Gorham and his council of elders had decided Jilly had become sufficiently competent to sail out, always within sight of other boats, on her own. That meant she should buy her own boat. preferably with a short-term loan from the Sconset Bank. Encouragement came from all sides. Most of the male sailors wanted to accompany Jilly on her trials.

Mayfield wrote on white paper: "All signals and drops as before. Center orders you remain in Nantucket or Boston. No domestic or foreign trips." Jilly read the message. Mayfield took the paper and burned it in an ash tray. Jilly turned and left. She took the Red Line to Harvard Square and walked to the lab.

MRS. CRUIKSHANK BENT over an ancient IBM typewriter while the messenger boy quietly placed large manila envelopes on her desk. The lab doors were closed. Jilly attacked the pile of miscellaneous paper on her desk. *Well*, she thought, *I am contracted for a year, and I'll fulfill that agreement, but this is probably the last night working for the Center.* That was sad, she concluded. *I am good at this sort of work. Technical proficiency, right age, good unwitting target, good cover here and on Nantucket. Krushkin made the right decision in assigning me here despite my lack of experience in the field. I haven't made any big mistakes. The Harry Black affair was unpredictable and outside the scope of the mission, but it was necessary. It's not the clever opposition making trouble, but the boobs who unwittingly insert themselves and destroy the rhythm of the operation.* She was coming to understood what it meant that every operation has a different rhythm. Many of them, it turned out, were not taught at Yasenevo.

She waited until Mrs. Cruikshank and the postdocs had left. The guard started his rounds. Jilly waited until he slipped into his routine, set her timer for seventeen minutes, and picked the lock on Ingraham's door. She inserted her thumb drive into the CPU, sat, and waited. A series of formulas spat across the monitor.

The encryption's format was familiar from her training at Yasenevo, not from her studies at the university. It seemed almost certain that Ingram had injected codes from a one-time pad. Jilly wondered if the one-time pad protected passwords for the entire file, some of the file, some parts of the file, or only his commentary, which he had written into a different file. Did another file exist, one that gave a clue to what the apparent one-time pad protected?

She opened other files that might be connected to Ingraham's main research and copied them. They, too, were encrypted. Time ran out, the guard would come around and notice Jilly's absence and her backpack sitting on her desk. She made sure the passwords were active and protected the files. She wrapped the drive in a plastic pouch and sealed it in a padded envelop. *I'll be damned if I'm going to give the crown jewel to Mayfield.* She used the emergency address in Chicago and wrote the lawn attendant's name at the tennis club as the return address. If the drive were not open opened according to the Center's instructions, it would self-erase. The material could possibly be recovered, but Diego wouldn't give it to any one with the skills needed to recover the data.

JILLY FINISHED two hour's work on the consistently profitable account of a State Street stock advisor's office. She relieved its staff of work for which they had little aptitude, and they always had coffee and sweet rolls waiting for her. She handed a disk to the plump middle-aged lady, told her the file's title, and left, leaving a trail of grateful smiles behind her. *Is there a school for well-paid ladies of a certain age who appear from nowhere to advise their nominal bosses on what is best for them? Well, they are pleasant enough and pay Mayfield on time.* These women seemed to buy their green, black and brown dresses from the same shop had probably schooled their children to buy Christmas and birthday gifts there, too. Their strands of pearls were sometimes three, but usually two. The pathologies resembled Charlie Banks's. Jilly concluded that there must be a born-and-bred class of attractive and agreeable men who are good at their jobs but lack the patience or inclination to keep their own affairs in an orderly condition. Like Philip and his office, she realized, capable people whose records were a shambles.

She walked easily to Park Square for the bus to Hyannis and ferried to Nantucket. She picked up her mail, left a check for Manuel, and searched her house. No signs of clandestine entry. *Either Horan has improved, or I have slipped a few notches on his list of priorities.* She lifted the bed's coverlet. The bed was not as she had made it. A tag for L. L. Bean dungarees lay on the sheet. Josito had graduated from the sofa to her bed. A can of oil was missing from the garage. She slept in her own bed and took the early plane to Logan.

CHAPTER 43

The Follower and His Demise

JILLY TOOK a quick inventory. The ears were the same, and so was the hunched-over gait. He swung his arms as before. HIs coat was dark, and he had shed his tie. He kept a respectful distance behind her and behaved so as to suggest he almost certainly was not the lead dog in a three-person surveillance. Jilly stopped at a long window. Only white clothes lay behind the window, and she could see the small man's reflection, the contours of his face, and a smile, peculiar to his craft, that shifted from giddiness to serious intent.

He moved from one display to another. The prices of the dresses were out of his shabby reach. They seemed to overwhelm and then displease him as he edged closer to Jilly. She resumed her walk and doubled back to the Marriott Hotel. He crossed to the opposite side of Arlington Street, waited for Jilly to pass, and recrossed to follow her on the same side. He's either a nutter, a stalker, or works for someone who can't pay for enough people to do a decent job. That eliminates the major services and the FBI.

The trouble was that a clumsy or awkward opponent could do more harm through stupidity than a trained professional who lay back and waited. She phoned Philip's office and told the voice mail that she was stuck in Malden. Whoever the trailer was, Jilly wanted to keep him away from Pinckney Street. She booked a room for two nights, showed her Harvard Security badge, and took an elevator to her room. It was clean, orderly, and lacked an attractive view of Boston or Cambridge. She unpacked her backpack and showered. She washed all scent off her. She wiped her face of lipstick and makeup. She took a thin rain coat with lightweight gloves in the right pocket out of her pack and slung a pocket book over her shoulder. She made sure her knife and ricin needle were on top of her clutter and easy to grasp even if she were knocked to the ground. The pocketbook opened with a simple twist of the clasp. It was seven o'clock.

Jilly opened the door and looked in the corridor's mirrors. There was no one. She descended to the lobby, went to the cafeteria, sat in a corner, and had a bowl of soup and iced tea. She paid with cash and left the hotel in the hope that she had flaunted herself enough to keep the creepy man alert and that his employer was willing to pay him overtime. She put on the gloves.

His reckless insistence on apparent pursuit annoyed Jilly for personal and mostly professional reasons. He was too present, too obvious, too unprofessional. She was prepared to deal with professional intelligence officers, but not with bumblers and incompetents. Jilly crossed Commonwealth Avenue and meandered down Exeter Street past the old theater building. She searched for an alley with two openings and a dumpster and prayed that the gods of civic duty did not watch over her. They did not. She circled around the block and ducked into the head of the alley. The man followed her and heard for the last time the voice of a woman: "I think you dropped something." The man bent over to pick up a piece of glass that clinked after Jilly had dropped it to the cement walkway.

The man wore a coat buttoned to his neck's bottom. Jilly thrust the blade past his shirt up and over the breast bone. The strength of Jilly's insertion was sufficient to push the man backwards. After that brief moment, he should have fallen forward so that he did not see his assailant and so his the blood fell only on him and the ground. Instead, he stood up and swung his body from side to side like a dog shaking after his bath. Some spatters hit Jilly as he backed away from her work. He man collapsed and stopped breathing. Jilly had carried wounded men in exercises, but this was the first time she had carried a body. She took the money from his wallet and left everything else.

The light in the alley reduced almost everything to shadows, but one promiscuous beam landed on the open wallet and identified the man as a private investigator licensed in the Commonwealth of Massachusetts. She grabbed the corpse under its shoulders from the rear and hoisted its trunk into the dumpster. When the Center of the body's weight was over the rim she lifted the legs and the dead man fell to the bottom of an empty container. His body thumped to the bottom. She looked inside at his ill-fitting clothes for the last time and closed the container's top. The dumpster had been empty, pickup probably wouldn't occur for a few days. In a few days the body would be discovered. In the meantime. worms would lunch.

There was also the problem of his blood on Jilly's clothes. She had to dispose of the gloves and the knife. The area would be searched once the body was decoded. Distance from the scene was imperative, and she could not be identified as someone who had been near the body that evening. She owned little self-doubt, even though her victim had never threatened her. In fact, they had never spoken. "I wonder how he sounded; stern, professional, forthright or meaching and bowed from the grief of his petty and failed life." She killed him to benefit the state and to further her mission. No more no less. But in the end his abrupt departure from life could scarcely benefit anyone. Bed with Phillip, and her dislike of anyone dogging her steps overlaid all. She knew that.

She strode out of the exit end of the alley and walked toward the river. There were fountains that let her wash off the most conspicuous stains. She remembered Olga Filipova's mantra that it is best to use cold water on a stain before it soaks into the fabric. The plastic rain coat cleaned easily, but her other clothes and shoes showed damage.

As she crossed Commonwealth Avenue, a policeman approached. He had soft brown eyes and a badge that said Menendez. "Are you all right, miss? Have you been hurt?" Jilly stumbled for a reply that would justify the blood stains and send the police officer, however solicitous, on his way. "Thank you, officer. I get nose bleeds. This is a bad one."

"Shall I call an ambulance for you? That's a lot of blood! Did someone hit you on the face?"

"No, officer, I'm fine now that those little blood vessels have all dried up. Thanks for the help." She moved an inch or two closer to him and smiled. Officer Menendez had seen beatings and this probably wasn't one. She walked straight, and she didn't have any facial bruises or defensive scratches on her hands. Domestic violence in this neighborhood of the prosperous and well educated always surprised him.

"OK, Miss." She strode away strongly. He examined her as someone he would have been happy to help. He was not a dumb cop.

My God, all that time at Yasenevo, at English House, with Helga and Lars, the nights with Philip, hung on a handsome police officer's excessive solicitousness and on my smile. English House, with Helga and Lars, Krushkin's dour brilliance, the chief's cynical world view had become nearly useless and worse, a burden under the policeman's kind enquiry. She turned the corner onto Commonwealth Avenue and got lost to the policeman's sight. She had killed a man fifteen minutes before. They had never spoken, and so far, she had gotten away with it. She hoped the cop wouldn't hear of the murder and put it together with the blood she had borne from the scene.

Krushkin was right. In a pinch, instinct trumped reason. Ridding herself of the knife and the money whose disappearance from the man's wallet was meant to indicate robbery was not part of the curriculum at Yasenevo. She put on gloves, ripped the money in pieces and threw them into different sewers near the esplanade. She washed blood off the knife as thoroughly as she could in the dim light. That consoled her, but in the end, she knew her attempt was futile—microscopic examination of the blade would yield the man's DNA and blood type. Still, she had done her best.

WHENEVER JILLY HAD VISITED the Hermitage, she stopped at Rembrandt's portrait of himself as an old man. As soon as she mounted the steps into that magical place, she said to no one in particular: "I'm here." She believed that the two yellow strokes down the left cheek certified the painter's genius and at the same time told the observer more about the tragedy of man that perhaps any wanted to know. She was proud her museum held one of the six self-portraits. "Would the old man approve of her life? Probably not," she whispered to herself.

He had admitted that the dark side existed and that its inhabitants were people like her. Understanding and sympathy, but no redemption, burst out of the painting.

"You brought all this on to yourselves" he was saying to viewers. Did he believe in it? Probably not, at least not when he put his brushes away. Yet he had lived to paint the portrait. Perhaps that by itself was a form of self-redemption. Jilly tilted her head toward no one in particular. "I don't think so.

SHE WALKED BACK to her hotel, turned up her raincoat's collar, said good evening to the porter, and went to her room. She spent an hour with every kind of hotel soap scrubbing the raincoat and shoes. She scrubbed herself in case she had missed a bit of tissue or blood that had fallen on her and that had not been washed off at the fountain. *So close to Philip, and yet so far. What would he or his colleagues or his ancestors conclude if they knew what their brave boy's latest mistress had accomplished that chilly night?*

In the morning, she mentioned a changed appointment at the front desk. The desk clerk cancelled her second night with a practiced smile and returned her credit card. She left the hotel and had a leisurely breakfast. She searched for a liquor store with customers, mostly habitual drinkers buying their day's supply of cheap whiskey. There were several cameras, and she did her best to put her back to them. One caught her full face. She bought a boxed bottle of moderately expensive vodka, as if for a gift. The Park Square ladies' room was inadequate for her purposes; it had cameras over the stalls and was too crowded. She boarded the bus to Hyannis. The vodka added weight to her back pack, but she was more conscious of the twelve-ounce knife than of anything else.

She could see, in her mind's eye, her victim's head swinging back and forth and his blood splashing onto her clothes and face. The man's death by itself did not trouble her while she was consummating it. He would have expected trouble and would have been paid to endure certain risks. He was a little man who had interfered in something bigger than himself. He had played a game for which he lacked the necessary skills. Jilly's operation had built a certain rhythm that boded a satisfactory end despite Mayfield's oafishness and Horan's questions. The man's death had upset that delicate pace. The possibility of being caught for having killed a bit player diminished with time and Jilly's distance from that dumpster.

ONCE ON BOARD the ferry, Jilly hurried toward the ladies room, found a stall, and sat down. She opened the bottle of vodka, soaked a sanitary pad with the liquid, and scrubbed the knife. She poured vodka over it so that every molecule of the man's substance was cleared away. *OK, now arrest me! I have nothing to hide.*

She washed her hands clean of the vodka and went up to the open deck. *Keep it or lose it? This is the blade that I trained on. Everybody knew I kept it in my room.* There had never been a drunken knock on her door because of its presence.

The knife had no hilt. *The balance and grip suit me perfectly.* At the end of the course, her instructor had presented it to her. He stood in front of her, almost at attention, and spoke formally: "You are my best student in many years. Take this. I hope that you never have to use it." She went aft to the stern and watched as the wake grew from the ferry's increased speed. She dropped the knife and then the bottle into the foam. The knife disappeared straightaway, the bottle floated for a moment before it sank.

THE WEEKEND brought minor delights and flatteries. The talk in Jed Gorham's circle, mostly laudatory, turned more often to the subject of her sailing skills and the possibility of her purchasing a suitable sailing boat. Jilly loved her new role as prey for her charming and intelligent friends. For the Nth time, several men had offered to find her a suitable craft and help her with the idiosyncratic twists that came with any boat. Jilly accepted their praise and promised to seek their assistance when she sailed into the mists off Monomoy Point.

She returned to her desk Sunday night and Monday to clean up some accounts that would bring checks from Mayfield. That relationship and its very useable stream were, she predicted, soon to end. Unpleasant persons should be shunned, the chief had advised. In the end, they interfere with success. Her hero Pushkin got too close to an enemy who killed him.

CHAPTER 44

Misunderstanding

THE MOWER WOKE her. The machine was cutting nonexistent grass, but Jilly was happy the boys had come. She had work to finish before her next trip to Boston and sandwiches to make for what had become a ritual lunch for three. She merged a bottle of near boiling water and rough tea to blend into something like the tea Olga Filipova fetched when Jilly came home from school. The fluid would turn dense during the morning and then cool in the refrigerator.

At noon, three instead of two appeared at the kitchen door. Manuel wore clean work clothes and had combed his black hair. He lacked his normal odor of gasoline and grass. The two boys skulked behind him. "Manuel, it is good to see you. Will you have lunch with us?

"No, Senhora Jilly. I have come with a sad burden."

"Oh dear, has one of your family died?"

"No, Senhora Jilly. I have come to tell you that my family says I may no longer work for you." His patriarchal stance suggested not anger but righteousness tinged with sadness. Jilly's face shrank.

"Why is that Manuel? Have I done something wrong?"

"Senhora, my son Manuelito has a book that you read with him. It says that a boy becomes a man when he buys beer for an older man. That is not true. It tells my son the wrong thing. A boy becomes a man when he marries and works enough to buy a house.Buying beer for others is not the advice I give Manuelito and Josito."

"Manuel, your son brought the book here, and I told him not to drink beer and not to buy beer for anyone else. That is my strong belief, and I gave both the boys that advice several times."

His face relaxed into acceptance. "I believe you, Senhora, and I will talk to the boys tonight. My brother is dead, and I am responsible for Josito." Manuel turned and left his two charges standing at the door. "I regret speaking to you about this matter, Senhora Jilly. We all like you."

"Thank you for your concern, Manuel." She and the boys sat down to their lunch. "After a lengthy silence, Jilly leaned into Manuelito's face: "Don't you ever drink beer or claim that I told you it's all right. Don't you ever talk about beer in this house. Bury it. Bring those books back to where you stole them from. Do you understand me?

Manuelito? And you too, Josito?" The littler one's swung above the ground, and when he nodded his whole body moved.

"That has been arranged, Senhora Jilly" Manuelito said shyly. They had not seen Jilly angry before. They nodded yes to her sermon and drank more iced tea. They rose from the table quietly. Manuelito stopped at the door and said, "Thank you, Senhora Jilly, for the lunch. We all like you."

"I will be away on Thursday. Do your regular job," she said with manufactured sternness. "Josito when you sleep on top of my bed make sure your clothes are clean and that you have washed your feet. Otherwise sleep on the sofa. "

She had surprised herself not so much by her anger as for her concern about the boys and Manuel's worries for them.

CHAPTER 45

Before Lunch

SHE LAY WITH HER BACK toward him. He breathed heavily, and she woke. Philip, she whispered to no one: "Do you think we have exhausted our potential? Do you think we have several rungs on the ladder left to climb? Do you think that I can do better than being a fixer-upper for other peoples' computer problems?"

"Have you been reading, Jilly?"

"What would happen if I left to accept a big money job in, say, Los Angeles?"

"My life would fall apart. Mrs. Cruikshank would run the entire office and lab spaces, Martha Hagedorn would crush me, and the stream of grants would dry up. I need you here, Jilly."

"That's very kind Philip." He had been out of character earlier, almost frisky while they played. *He has taken a decisive and favorable step in his life. A new grant? Has he found someone else? I'm on Nantucket weekends, he must get bored. What if I loved him and got jettisoned like the others? What if he loved me and asked me to stay? Could I betray my new friend Krushkin?*

"Jilly when you are away I dream of you in the kitchen, in bed, disparaging my wine, or just walking toward me. I go on a high, and I think of my work."

Philip are you saying that my absence helps you discover things? That I must be away for you to concentrate? I don't like that. It is the opposite for me, you distract when you are around."

"No, it is just that vintages are impossible to predict. In most places, even PhDs see science as the science they have been taught. I see science as connecting an infinity of dots in an unending space whose end we shall never see. I begin to see dots beyond the edge of my work that I didn't know existed. I look for A and find X, Y, and Z. Then I try to connect them. Some want to connect and some seem unable or unwilling to mate with any of their colleagues. I practice the Science of the Night, as François Jacob puts it.

My post docs' minds do not roam so freely. They take a pile of puzzle pieces and put them together with as much logic as they can bring to bear. Pieces with autumn leaves go together. Pieces with ocean go together. That is Jacob's Science of the Day. Sometimes I think they are searching for self-confirmation, for what they know or like. It gets you jobs and tenure. I live in a world they and sometimes I cannot see. Reason gets you so far; intuition or whatever you call it, if it is working right, leads you to strange places where you can begin to use reason. Often I find what I do not like. Science is not always symmetrical, the thing of beauty that its practitioners claim. Sometime its inferences are horrible beyond thinking.

"But Jillian, though my mind wanders to dots when you are away, often good dots, I always want you back before you leave. Before we doze off again, I want to tell you that I am looking at the most beautiful left ear in the universe. I want it to stay where I can see it." Their feet touched at the foot of the bed and Philip fell asleep.

"PHILIP, THIS IS THE BEST coffee ever." He had dressed early. An unusual energy pervaded the kitchen. There was a sense of division between past and future. Philip exuded a sense of triumph. He was prince and Jilly a serving wench. She did not approve. Before he bolted out the door, Jilly informed Philip that she was to have lunch with Charlie Banks at the Harvard Club on Commonwealth Avenue.

"Who is Banks" he mumbled?

"He is my lawyer and a dear friend from Nantucket. He is a bachelor. He has gotten me some good accounts, and he helped me out during a very complicated part of my life. How could you forget? He is very practical and down to earth. As far as I know, he's not intimate with germs of any kind. You probably wouldn't like him."

"Well, I hope the lunch is ok. You can never tell about places like that, although I hear the lobster is very good."

"We will see, my dearest Philip."

THREE PAINTINGS at the Gardner that that were not there, paintings that I will probably never see, brought me into a life as far from Yasenevo as could be dreamed of. What would Pushkin or her father or Olga Filipova advise when Jilly found herself excluded from the professor's life? *Is he meeting her for lunch in Cambridge while I'm with Charlie on the island? Have I missed something about his weekend plans? Will the postdocs tell me if I've become the fifth wheel on the wagon?*

Her contract with Wolpe had a long way to go. But it would be awkward to continue working on his progress reports and to reconcile his personal checking account and business accounts. *I would make a scene when I saw what he spends on her. It would take a new person months to arrive at a working knowledge of his life in paper. His stack of hen scratchings and illegible notes to self will grow back to its original height. Where would I sleep when I came to Boston? A dreary hotel whose blandness is exceeded only by its cost? A red leather sofa at The Athenaeum? Would we cross paths at the Gardner? What would we say? Nothing? Do you still wash the pots and pans after each meal with her?*

She left Pinckney Street alone. The business at hand was a monthly session at a wealthy extended family's private office. Their attorneys, three men and two women, all elderly, handled a gaggle of relatives whose investments, tax returns, theater tickets, airplane reservations and major purchases exceeded their will or capacity to manage.

One of the men bought a new overcoat every four years. Size remained constant. Color and style were left to one of the lawyers. The attorneys and their clients had, in many cases, been classmates. The details of divorces, illegitimate children, and disastrous investments would have filled the newspapers with scandal for weeks had they been known. Jilly had been made to sign a confidentiality agreement as part, perhaps the most important, of her contract.

All five attorneys showed great surprise when confronted by Jilly's accurate compilations of this and that income, expense, and donation. One imprudent young man had bought an island near Jamaica that turned out not to exist. He was referred to as "the young Mr. David." The elder Mr. David had earned enough money to permit his son to diminish the family's wealth in his green years by a not inconsiderable amount. His unmarried cousin, now a proper and handsome lady of a certain age, visited Philadelphia every month for years beyond counting. She was not married and no one at The Office asked her the purpose of her trips. That, it was explained to Jilly, was not The Office's concern. All such outlays were to fall under the words "personal business expenses" and claimed as deductions on her federal and state tax returns. The Office had not suffered an audit by the federal government or the Commonwealth of Massachusetts for many years. The partners took this as a sign of their prudence and delicacy in handling family affairs. One member of the family sent five-thousand dollars each quarter to an individual whose name was different from his. Jilly came to believe that the man was an illegitimate son. His name was never mentioned in conversation or in other correspondence. Jilly had known nothing of such matters before she arrived in America.

CHAPTER 46

Confessions

JILLY WALKED across the Common slowly. She had a good fifteen minutes to spare. She had left her comfort zone with its churches and libraries for a place she had never known. Charlie had dangled an invitation for a meal in front of Jilly for months. She had never accepted, partly out of an unnecessary loyalty to Philip, but mostly because she and Charlie had never been in Boston at the same time or had conflicting appointments if they were. This time, though, he seemed particularly insistent, and she finally found herself agreeing to see him in town.

How will the women be dressed? Will a pants-suited working girl embarrass Charlie or pass unnoticed? She entered, and a porter immediately sprung up from nowhere to ask her business. She mentioned her lunch with Charlie at one o'clock. The porter disappeared, and Charlie was brought forth. He was not wearing the five-year-old gray suit that hung off him. Still, his tie wandered outside his jacket as he kissed Jilly on the cheek. "Let's go upstairs and chat quietly before we eat."

He escorted Jilly up a flight of stairs and down a poorly lit corridor. "Charlie, what are those two great bulbs outside the front door? Do they really light up?"

"Yes, but it's noontime now. Consider a gray day just before Christmas. You have past wives, children, and grandchildren. You haven't bought Christmas presents for them, and you really don't want to go to the trouble. You don't like them. Those lights are a beacon of hope, guides to a better life inside the door to this quiet and safe existence."

"Charlie, do you have ex-wives and grandchildren?"

"Thank heaven, no, Jilly."

"I didn't think so."

He opened a door to a small room with three easy chairs surrounding a sullen coffee table. "Jilly, I've wanted to have this discussion for some time. Things simply haven't worked out."

My God, is someone suing me? Has Philip's wife brought the wrath of the Biology Department and its secretaries down on me? Charlie got me my business license. Did he make a mistake?

"Jilly, please don't take what I am about to say as a criticism—either direct or implied. I am sure that you act from your own best interests. But it's important for me to know why you concluded that you had to kill Harry Black and that poor dimwitted

PI the other week." Banks paused to give Jilly the opportunity for recollection like a priest dealing with a recalcitrant penitent. She had buried both events as necessary for a successful completion of her mission and advancement to a higher position than those of Mayfield and several others in the Sluzhba, all of whom she despised.

"I didn't kill anyone. What are you talking about?" Her training took over. She did not cross her legs or wring her fingers. She maintained a conversational tone in her replies. She kept her seat and back in place.

"I AM BEING UNFAIR to you, Jilly. Let me tell you a long story as briefly as I can. I am half Russian. My father met a beautiful ballet dancer from the Mariinski on a student trip. They had a baby to whom they gave a Russian name. I have buried that name deep in my subconscious. My father returned to the States to go to law school and left me in my mother's care. He graduated and worked for Ropes, Green for the rest of his life.

"But mother argued that I interfered with her career and would, in any case, be better off in America. She was right, those were bad days in Russia. Lousy food, little medical care, and cold flats. My mother traveled, too, and that made things worse for me because I was always shuttled off to relatives and friends while my mother danced in Omsk and Kiev.

"She was not a great dancer like the Bessmertnaya sisters, but she ended up as nachalnik (boss) of the Corps de Ballet in Petersburg. I went to grade school here. My father took me to my mother's for a month every summer. Starting when I was twelve, my father would pick me up from my boarding school, and I would stay with her the entire summer. I grew up bilingual. I had to make sure I spoke with a prep school accent when I got back each fall. All said, I hated the political system there, but I liked the people. Still do. One of my summer playmates, I called Iggy."

He's known about me all along? And from the inside! She yelled, "You grew up with Krushkin?"

"Yes, and I believe we still think well of each other. We played on the same soccer team. I was the goalie. He grew fast. He had a massive chest when I was still a skinny kid. He never made fun of my American accent and after each game, he would tell me where I and the team had made missteps. When I made a mistake, he punched me in the stomach. He is a brilliant man.

"He asked me to do little things for him at first, then we agreed that I was fit for more sophisticated matters. I went to law school, passed the Massachusetts bar exam, clerked in a good firm to learn the ropes, and settled here. When you were posted, Iggy activated me to keep a watchful eye on his protegee working in the field for the first time. Yes, we did have some counter surveillance on you—more to keep you out of trouble than anything else." Banks stopped and waited in vain for Jilly's thanks. "The Harry Black affair was difficult for us to understand and justify. Why Jilly?"

SHE SPUTTERED out her story: "Harry knew, or thought he knew, that I was stealing intellectual property from my clients and selling it to the highest bidder. He concluded that I stole test results from drug companies or from research labs and sold them to other drug companies. He had the right idea, but the wrong target. He wanted access to my body and my files or he would denounce me as a common thief. He had to go, Charlie. He was a babbling fool and a real danger to the mission. I executed a very professional end to Harry's existence. There have been no repercussions. The coroner, the medical examiner, and the hearing judge were all satisfied. They had no alternative theory to inject into that mess. You were there by my side the whole time. You knew everything but the truth. His elimination advanced my life. Yours, too. You were a splendid companion during those days. You will always have my gratitude."

Jilly leaned back into the very comfortable men's club chair. There was a lengthy silence. Charlie sat as prosecutor, judge, and jury. "You know, being close to another Russian who speaks my language, I am starting to think in Russian terms rather than English phrases. Very dangerous."

"It surely is, but I have managed to cope with that paradox, and so will you. The difficulty comes when you are in a room full of Poles, Czechs, or Ukrainians. The Slavic cloud descends over you, and you enter the misty world of Rurik, the Mongols, and Catherine the Great. I get sentimental. When I hear the old language, I compare Sochi, where my mother lives, to Nantucket, where I live."

"Where do you come out, Charlie, Sochi or Nantucket?"

"The lobsters are splendid here, Jilly. Now that I have heard the whole story, I think you did the right thing."

"You should have had more trust. It was Harry or me. Nobody misses him much. anyway."

"I agree. He was not a nice man. His death advanced my life as well as yours."

There was a knock on the door. "Come on in, PJ."

CHAPTER 47

The End

THE DOOR OPENED and Philip James Ingraham joined them. "Katya Michailovna, your father has always claimed that you are an outstanding young lady, and how right he is." He bent over and kissed a frozen Jilly on her cheek.

"PJ, we have just finished discussing some of the operational details. Jilly gets a clean sheet. Now we have shocked her again. She is still beautiful, but she can't speak."

Jilly made a gargling sound that bore no relation to any known language and pointed accusingly at Ingraham. "You bastard" finally emerged.

"Now, Jilly, wait until you've heard PJ's side of the whole story. I think you will conclude that this little slice off the history of germs will benefit all three of us." Charlie raised his hand in benediction of the words he had just offered to Jilly. "We appreciate the part you played and the risks you ran more than we can ever say. You are the hero your father and Iggy said you would be." Charlie waved a dismissive wave and turned to Ingraham: "PJ, you know the whole story better than I. Why don't you take over?"

"Jilly, I met Charlie when I was a graduate student and he was in law school. Somehow, good chemistry I guess, we kept in touch, and Charlie has handled my personal affairs since he opened shop. He kept them in a box separate from the rest. You never saw them when you toted up his monthly billings.

"Jilly, I met your father at one of the few conferences in the West he deigned to attend. He mentioned you in almost every sentence. He was besotted with his only child, and he wanted the best that life could offer you. Even then, he judged that you were not a scientific researcher, but that you were very bright and might explore some interesting opportunities that would cast glory on him and propel you into a position of power and influence. He wanted you to leave the drab bureaucracy of Petersburg and fly off to something better. My fellow alumni in New York keep me informed what certain people look for to advance their national interests. Every Russian spook at the UN broadcast that Moscow wanted anything they could find about germ warfare. Making a deal with them wasn't difficult. Putting you, PJ, and me together was a bit complicated, but it worked.

"By the way, Krushkin's tests and your record at Yasenevo supported your father's view of your potential. From your father to Comrade V to Yasenevo's awful commandant to the Chief at English House to Ignats, who plucked the right candidate from a group of bright, but unimaginative students. Well, plucked is not the right word. He'd had a hand in placing you there. We began to conclude you are a winner." The room with its dark green walls grew smaller and smaller as Jilly heard of her father's long reach, which had created her present incarceration with her two masters.

"THE SOONER I GET that lobster, the better, Jilly. Let's make a long story short! Germ warfare is a massive industry—probably as large and intimidating as the nuclear business, which I always thought was crude and lacked direction. Washington could never say how many people a bomb would kill, a million or ten million. The big countries spend billions to stay up to date with other big countries.

"You remember our discussion once about how ideas come to me, how scientists make discoveries? I found by chance a method of bacterial warfare whereby small or big targets could be eliminated at will by the perpetrator. Wolpe didn't predict this outcome. My work is my own. I attach a description of the method to my experiment, but no one can duplicate my work for now. Maybe Jacob in Paris or lownie at Cambridge. Some years I'm ahead, some years they are. Right now, I am years ahead of the others. Jacob likes long lunches. Lownie at Cambridge is hard at work, but he likes to travel. There are traps, false leads and blind allies that will take years to eliminate. Meantime, I have tucked away all the years of summer salary the foundation has provided, so I might buy a house in Nantucket. There are some other funds, too. Yes, I will buy that house. Wolpe will examine my results and claim they are so brilliant and complex that few can understand their fullness.

"I, and my colleagues in Russia, have researched ways of pinpointing targets so that we kill or disable the target with little or no collateral damage. Why kill kids because their daddy is a bad person? .The Russian scientists were and are under pressure to hurry with a toxin or a bug that could be planted and set off later at a specific time. I don't work that way. In any case, the Kremlin took no chances. They wanted the Sluzhba to mount an operation against my lab. Iggy received unsubtle notes that his tenure was at stake.

"You, my dear, were assigned to be the point on the spear. Despite hiccups from Mayfield and the mousy PI, you succeeded. Krushkin keeps his job and his southern dacha, and we are adequately compensated for the hours we devoted to the tasks at hand. To be sure, the data we sent to the Center is incomplete, but we are all rug merchants at heart. One of us observed as you hoisted that wretched man into the dumpster. You are very strong. You may have noted that Mrs. Cruikshank has been absent for a few days. She carried an encrypted version of my results to the Wolpe Foundation in Chicago. No hackers that way.

"Now here's where you come in. You retrieved, very artfully I must say, a truncated version of my final results. That is what you sent to your emergency drop. That was wise. Mayfield was a dreadful man at the end of his usefulness. That version will satisfy my colleagues in your country. The fuse is not complete. It needs six months of work and some attention to the frequencies they need to set off the device. Engineering of the fuse itself is not my field. and I leave the solution of that rather insignificant problem to my friends in other disciplines."

"So you are not only a complete bastard but a traitor to your country."

"No, I passed on material to you that will fill the package but does no more than offer a heads up on the fusing because our countries both want to neutralize bad little men who do not think rationally. Harry Black comes mind. Nothing you sent will lead them off track. It will just not get them to the top of the mountain as fast as a complete accounting would."

"You're a double bastard, Philip."

"No, I AM NOT, and I will explain why. A couple of years ago, I was ordering a drink at the faculty club when a man from the Emirates began to chat. He hadn't just run into me by chance. He spoke English with an Oxford accent and had a scientific background. It was soon obvious where the conversation was headed. I broke off, and we nodded each time we passed.

"I told Charlie about the incident and gave him the fellow's particulars. Also not completely by chance, he ran into this fellow at the bar at the Harvard Club in New York. They talked and promised to have a drink or lunch in the near future. Charlie implied he was something other than he is. It was clear after the second iced tea that this man wanted to buy western research on behalf of parties unknown. At that point, Charlie told him flat out that he lived on Nantucket, where he practiced civil law and knew none of the heads of the companies in which the man with the Oxford accent might be interested. Charlie discussed the possible alternatives with me before his next trip to New York.

"We agreed that we needed answers to two questions: What did this man want and could he pay? Charlie returned to New York, and after much iced tea, he brought back two affirmative responses. Charlie checked the banks through some old friends. The man was either very rich or had very rich friends. We decided it was the latter and that he was acting on behalf of principals whose identities he chose not to disclose.

"Charlie let the buyer know he had found him information from a source other than the companies the man had mentioned and negotiated the quantity and quality of the germ data that he would fetch up, the method of delivery, and the price. All seemed satisfactory to us until you came along, the new superstar in Iggy's firmament. We had to decide whether to take you into our confidence or wait until the operations were complete. We decided to keep you unwitting of both operations."

"Charlie, you were most fortunate. For a moment I thought you were getting too close to my many lives, especially when I began my relationship with this creepy bastard." Jilly pointed a finger of scorn at her employer with the awful wife. "At one point after the Black business, I considered that Charlie might be preparing to blackmail me and that I might be forced to take steps."

"I'm glad you made the right decision, Jilly. I value my life. I hope you and Philip value it, too."

INGRAM ROSE and tried to pace the room. He failed; the room was too small for his lengthy stride. "Jilly, we all hungry, and I will shorten this sad tale with a happy ending. The ripe fruit of my research went to Wolpe, who will do God knows what with it. Probably return it to the drug company that provided the original funding, maybe to a startup in Silicon Valley for more money than they paid me. You sent a limited file to Moscow. I know the lads who will be tasked with figuring out the formulas that I left out. They'll fix it, but over a very long time. Trouble is, we all think alike in this small community. They may guess at what I have done.

"Back to our prospective buyer from the Harvard Club bar. Charlie told him that he had learned that my research was not as advanced as it truly was. The man replied that his principals would take what they could get and pay handsomely. And so they did. They paid twenty-five-million dollars for an incomplete file. It had so many experimental options and blind alliest that it will take years for the buyers to unravel. Charlie told them that up front. They replied that their French contacts could handle any germ task that came their way. Maybe not. What you sent Krushkin was far less incomplete.

"Charlie delivered three thumb drives to his acquaintance. At the same time, the money was deposited in the proverbial Swiss bank. Fifteen million to my account, I did the heavy lifting after all, five million to Charlie, and five million to you for your very astute management of the bumps in your road. You performed well, Jilly. And don't worry, nobody knows who you are."

"Fine, you're only a half-bastard. Which bank and what's the code for my account?"

"Later Jilly, we are all wanting those lobsters."

Ingraham motioned Charlie to leave the room. He grabbed Jilly and squeezed her up against him. "Jilly, I meant all those words I said to you at Pinckney Street. I want you!"

Jilly's body half responded. "We'll discuss that later, Philip."

SHE OPENED THE DOOR and followed Charlie Banks, who stood at the top of the stairs. They sat, and a young man with deep brown eyes and a scar in front of his right eye served three small lobsters and a bottle of good Moselle. There was no conversation. The glasses were drained. They passed on dessert and finished their second glasses of iced tea. At the meal's end, Charlie looked at Jilly until she nodded for him to speak. "Jilly, I thought you might be interested in news from the home front."

"Go on, Charlie."

"You won't be bothered by Mayfield. Did you hear his sadness?

"No."

"A hit and run driver plowed into Jerry on Dartmouth. He didn't make it to Mass General. No one could identify the driver. One old man said it was a blue sedan, the plates were covered with mud, and the driver looked like a comedian. He had bulbous eyes and hair down below his brows, rather like the man who visited you and Horan on Nantucket. We assume he was the same. The car hit Jerry and threw him into an old lady who carried a shopping bag. The bag broke and out came two kilos of cocaine. It seems that she was the neighborhood messenger girl. Some risk that it will take them a while to figure out who the Center's new Boston facilitator is, but also a clean slate."

"No!"

"A car fitting that description was found burned out behind a brothel in Revere. By the way, the man you knew as 32 made too many mistakes. He was sent home and now translates American newspapers in the First Directorate's basement. Every morning he translates the first page of the New York Times and reads it to the First Director's chief. The dentist who did your work was interrogated, nothing found. Same with Lars, who is engaged to a wealthy widow. She has promised to buy him a new boat when they marry. Jacobsson was too well known as a petty crook. The police ignored him.

A few months after you left to return to English House for your last briefing, the German police picked up Helga. Nothing to do with you. She was tried and given probation. The Germans had known her occupation all along, but they found nothing they could use to put her away—she had acquired and burned her Stasi files. She retired on a good pension from us and several weeks ago married a wealthy German gentleman with a good name. They are restoring his family castle on the Neckar. He is older than she. They are expecting as we speak."

"I liked Helga," Jilly commented quietly. Charlie smiled at Jilly, and they rose with more than perfunctory thanks to their waiter.

"PJ, LET ME TELL YOU something that comes via my work as your personal attorney, not from my being the bank's chief counsel. Yesterday, I received a letter from Martha Hagedorn's attorney to the effect that Martha's relationship with her horses' groom precludes a family relationship with you. You are a free man."

"At last! Thank God!"

Charlie signed the credit card receipt. "I think we did rather well," he commented. "Something else Jilly. Our work will, in the long run benefit investors everywhere. The three of us have created a new product, my research, that has been circulated world over in three versions. That fact will shortly be known to clever people on Wall St. A few will buy the whole piece, most will buy what they think are the juicy parts. The pieces will become smaller and smaller. Many will be traded very frequently London,

Zurich, Wall St. who knows in the hope of huge profits. We three have created a secondary market of apparently great, but really transitory value. Money will be made, a few young men will become partners all because each of us contributed according to his or her talents. You never thought that you would become a successful capitalist did you Jilly?"

"Remember Jilly, Jed knows nothing about this situation. Without being aware, he does us many favors. He and his wife like you."

"That is what I intended to have happen all along, Charlie. But tell me, what the hell is that package you've been fondling like a newborn baby?"

"I almost forgot, Jilly. I knew you might be vacationing in Europe soon—seeing to bank matters and visiting France and Italy. We chipped in and bought you this book. It's very good. I read it myself. It's The Guide to Baroque Rome by a highly respected critic, Anthony Blunt. The name of your Swiss bank is the Banque Lucerne de Breau. Your account number is coded inside the book. You'll find it."

"Thank you, Charlie. Close friends shouldn't have secrets among themselves."

ONE OF THE GIRLS at English House had shouted the word farce too many times, probably without knowing its meaning. Piqued, Jilly looked it up in the House's English language dictionary: "A dramatic work intended only to excite laughter, often by presenting ludicrously improbable events."

"My God," she whispered to herself, "I'm a minor actress in a farce."

Charlie was pondering. "I wonder if anything like this is coming our way again, PJ"

"I'm sure it will." Ingraham replied sagely. "It's inevitable, Of all the molecules floating around the known and unknown universes, at least some are bound to benefit us. Charlie, you'll make sure that happens, won't you. Preferably with private clients. We all know that a thing does not exist unless it is stolen. Best we let friend Krushkin retire without such matters on his mind."

"Of course. As long as we have Jilly on our side."

"Jilly?" they asked together.

"I will not be devoured by two mendacious monsters."

"Of course not Jilly. Sometimes we astonish even ourselves, but we are almost always right. In these matters you are our equal, our friend and our trusted partner. We trust you as I hope you trust us.

"One last thing before we part. Should one of us buy some good shirts and ties for Ignats?"

"I will" Jilly answered. "I can guess his collar size and sleeve length better than either of you, and I'll match the ties to the shirts. Nobody else has done that for the poor fellow."

Epilogue

JILLY MADE her weekly call to the secure number in Venice. A disemboweled American voice answered. The reply was not routine. The voice ordered Jilly to end her holiday. She was to tell the airline that she would not be able to use her return ticket to America because she had met an old friend and had decided to extend her museum tour. She to fly to Prague using her American name and passport and to tell no one inside or outside the service. Once in Prague she was to wait in the arrival lounge for further orders.

Why? Those bastards. I needed the break. Medals bore me. I want time in Rome for Bernini's sculptures and good food.

HER MONTH-LONG HOLIDAY disappointed her regular clients who were assured that Jilly would catch up with their work on her return. The trip was her reward her to the brilliant success in Boston, but it was clear that Krushkin approved of her vacation from Nantucket. Only Philip mourned her absence. No further assignment had been given her. No security problems had arisen during her time spent transferring Philip's findings to the Center. The tap was off her phone. The FBI man had either found nothing against her or had simply walked away from the case. His lack of pestering gave Jilly, for the moment, a clean bill of health.

For months on Nantucket and in Boston she had acted almost mindlessly as a tool of the state. Even with Philip, she acted like a gaggle of molecules expertly programmed to perform certain tasks. She had a certain discretion as to how she executed her orders, but in reality she had no freedom. Every moment was directed at the success of her mission, and if that failed preservation of her life.

The days traveling from Switzerland to Italy had given her more pleasure than her sailing days in Denmark. She visited the Banque de Breau in Lucerne. On the advice of her banker, who resembled an aging remnant of the Hitler Jugend she bought four million dollars of gold bonds and put one million in Euros into a safe deposit box. Although she could not yet spend her reward conspicuously, she withdrew two-hundred thousand in Euros. The train passed over the mountains onto the northern Italian plain and then to Rome. She chose an excellent, but not luxurious hotel near the Borghese Gardens and shopped. During the first three days of her visit, the Via del Popolo saw a young American lady with excellent taste choosing splendid outfits to be shown to her friends in Boston as proof of her forays into the heart of Renaissance and Baroque Europe. She had decided to upscale her Boston business and bought a few dresses suitable for meeting Boards of Directors. After displaying herself in a shop's mirrors, she bought one black evening dress so elegant that it would probably pass unnoticed by the wives of winter Nantucket. She bought another for own small parties. The Berninis in Rome seen from just a few feet away came to life and gave her a new quiet ecstasy. The catalogue images from her days in Petersburg faded in the light of the reality. Even the delights at Pinckney Street and Philip's loving attentions grew faint. She lived in another world, forgetting to eat until evening. She recalled once asking Krushkin what would happen if she ran. He predicted a dire end. Probably he did not realize that she could be found in any one of a few dozen churches and museums.

In Rome, she had little trouble adjusting to the chic aspect of Roman women. Everything about her suggested a handsome woman of means traveling alone and unapproachable. She checked out of her hotel early. The clerk did not examine her, muttered sympathy, and inserted her credit card into the recorder. She signed, rolled her suitcase out to the sidewalk, waited, and took the bus for Fiumicino.

SHE CLEARED the security line. The agent regarded her with bare civility, and she boarded the plane with a crowd of dingy businessmen, raggedy students, and a few old people probably visiting their home villages after years or decades away. The flight took little time. The landing was bumpy. A crosswind, the pilot said. His accent was vague but middle European, not the confidence inspiring all-American parlance of the pilots around Nantucket.

She walked carefully down stairs that were neither Russian nor American in their capacity to hold a normal shoe. A classless Eurocrat stamped her passport; a shaggy scarred man found her baggage. She waited in the arrivals arena. Long sheds lay in the distance, and she wondered if they served as lazar houses for dead protesters all laid out for disposal. The Czech Internal Service had a reputation at Yasnevo for efficiency. *Or are they warnings for arriving passengers to behave?*

In moment she spotted the man who was sent to pick her up. He could be no one else, small, sallow faced and stooped with thinning hair. He wore an ill-cut gray suit that would be odd on a western European but fit for the man he was. His eyes had blue pupils, and where the whites should have been was overlaid with a sickly yellow. He might have been a professor at a provincial university struck down with a fell disease that had gone untreated. He need not be seen to be disliked.

He stopped in front of Jilly, gave a false smile and offered equally inauthentic greetings. "Welcome to Prague, Jillian. We are happy you answered our request so quickly. I am Pavel Grishkin You may call me Pete. Please come with me. We have a car waiting for you."

Her defensive apparatus raced into overdrive. Inside Russia, only Krushkin and the Chief of English House were allowed knowledge of her work name. Pete walked ahead of Jilly and offered no help with her baggage. They went outside to an ordinary brown car with Czech license plates. The driver was a burly man whose head almost touched the car's ceiling. He did not turn his head or ask for directions. He drove slowly toward the airport's exit and suddenly turned down a small road that led to a distant hangar.

"We need you back in Moscow, Jillian. We have a plane waiting for you." His voice had a meeching cast. The dullest eye of any intelligence operative could see he was a security man who would go no further in his career. Obsequiousness varnished by the rank of his superiors was his defense against the world.

Pete's car brought her to an outlying dirt strip. He slumped against the seat without words and seemingly without breathing. The car stopped at the end of the field. The driver yanked open Pete's door; Jilly opened her own and grabbed her baggage. Pete directed her to a waiting two-engine prop plane. The paras had used it in Afghanistan. It was an old Antonov. Dirt obscured the camouflage. Pete steered Jilly to the iron steps at the airplane's starboard fuselage, then pushed her and her baggage inside. It stank of sweat. The seats were canvas. Barely protected low-wattage bulbs swung on their cords from overhead. "You may sit anywhere, but fasten your seat belt tightly. This a rough dirt field, and we are taking off into a storm."